Carol Matas

Jesper

Scholastic Canada Ltd.
Toronto New York London Auckland Sydney
Mexico City New Delhi Hong Kong Buenos Aires

Scholastic Canada Ltd.
175 Hillmount Road, Markham, Ontario L6C 1Z7, Canada

Scholastic Inc.
555 Broadway, New York, NY 10012, USA

Scholastic Australia Pty Limited
PO Box 579, Gosford, NSW 2250, Australia

Scholastic New Zealand Limited
Private Bag 94407, Greenmount, Auckland, New Zealand

Scholastic Ltd.
Villiers House, Clarendon Avenue, Leamington Spa,
Warwickshire CV32 5PR, UK

Library and Archives Canada Cataloguing in Publication
Matas, Carol, 1949-
Jesper / Carol Matas.
First published: Toronto : Lester & Orpen Dennys, 1989.
ISBN 0-439-95639-0
1. World War, 1939-1945--Underground movements--Denmark--
Juvenile fiction.
I. Title.
PS8576.A7994J48 2005   jC813'.54   C2004-906878-4

6 5 4 3 2 1   Printed in Canada   05 06 07 08 09

OTHER BOOKS BY CAROL MATAS:

ACKNOWLEDGEMENTS

Heartfelt thanks to:

Per Brask, my husband, who inspired this story with tales of his father's and grandfather's exploits in the resistance. Also for his invaluable help while we were in Denmark — as a guide, interpreter, and (not to be overlooked) spelling expert. And for his listening and commenting, draft by draft.

Inge and Olaf Brask, my in-laws, who patiently told me all about life in Denmark during the Second World War and who read the manuscript and answered my constant questions so as to ensure verisimilitude.

Perry Nodelman, who also read the manuscript draft by draft — taking time away from his own hectic schedule — to give me criticism that was always clear, concise, and most important, right. I can't thank him enough.

George Szanto, for his thoughtful critique.

The many Danes who made the time and took the trouble to talk to me; it would be impossible to mention all of them here.

The Manitoba Arts Council, which made the entire project possible with the award of a Major Arts Grant that gave me the means to travel to Denmark and the time to write the book.

FOREWORD

The Second World War began on September 1, 1939, when the German army attacked Poland. Although Germany had been expanding aggressively for some years, Britain and France had hoped that peace could somehow be maintained. But Poland was their ally, and when that country was invaded they had no choice: Both declared war.

On April 9, 1940, the German army invaded Denmark and Norway. Denmark fell within the day; Norway resisted but was conquered within a month. These countries, and eventually France, Belgium, The Netherlands and most of Europe, became "occupied" lands — controlled and exploited by the Germans, and able to fight back only within secret, highly dangerous "resistance" movements.

Carol Matas's novel *Lisa* told the story of a young Jewish girl who followed her brother,

Stefan, into the Danish resistance and fell in love with a resistance fighter named Jesper. Together they took part in dangerous and important operations.

On October 1, 1943, the Germans tried to round up Denmark's Jews and ship them to concentration camps. Word of the plan slipped out, and most Jews — including Stefan and Lisa — escaped to Sweden in a daring and well-planned operation. But Jesper was not Jewish, so he was able to stay behind in Denmark — and he and the resistance continued their desperate campaign . . .

1

I am to be executed. It will be soon. The Nazis are getting desperate, and as they get more desperate they get meaner.

I've been alone in this cell for two weeks now. There is a little desk in the corner, and a few minutes ago a guard came in and dropped a piece of paper and a pencil on the desk. I'm allowed one last letter, a farewell letter to my family. The guard laughed. He knows I can't write. They pulled all my fingernails out and my fingers are swollen and bleeding. But I can think. They can't stop that.

It was the guy in the cell to the left of mine who gave me this idea. We pass messages every day by Morse code, tapping on the wall. Yesterday I asked him what he was doing to keep from going crazy. He told me he was composing poems and then memorizing them. Well, I tried yesterday. It didn't work. I used to write poetry all the time, but now I can't. Then I thought of another idea. I'll think back over everything that's happened and put it in order. If by some miracle I live, I'll write it all down. And if I die, it will have kept me busy for my last few days. I don't want to become morbid or afraid. I don't want to despair.

I wish my fingers wouldn't throb. It's so hard to concentrate. But maybe as I think, as I try to get it all straight, I'll forget about the pain — if I think hard enough. I'll try not to look at my hands; somehow they hurt more when I look at them. They remind me of something, though — a scene I can picture so clearly, as if it happened a few minutes ago. I see my hands and they aren't bloody or torn. They're soft and they're cupped, because I'm holding a pile of sugar in them.

It was April of 1940, only three days after the Germans invaded Denmark. My best friend, Stefan, and I were carrying out our first act of resistance. We were both fourteen then. Fourteen and angry and ashamed. Denmark had surrendered to Germany without a fight. But that didn't mean *we* couldn't fight. Just the opposite. Of course, we had no weapons, no contacts — we really didn't know what we were doing. But there were German vehicles everywhere — cars and transport trucks — so Stefan, who's always had a scientific turn of mind, suggested that a little sugar in their gas tanks would help slow the Germans down. These days sugar is so scarce that it's like gold, but back then we bought big bags at the store.

We decided to make our first hit after school. We raced our bicycles home, filled our pockets with sugar, then rode downtown. We parked our bikes near Dagmarhus, a large office building just across from the town hall square. The Nazis had taken it over as their headquarters. Then we sauntered up and down the streets checking out enemy positions. I had never been so excited in my life. I really wasn't scared. I figured we were much smarter than those locusts — we called them that because of their green uniforms — or, if all else failed, much faster. It's true my heart was pounding so hard I could barely hear Stefan as he whispered to me, but that was more excitement than fear. Stefan walked past a big German truck and motioned to me. Then he paused just by the gas tank and pretended to look for something in his jacket. He took out a small notebook from his shirt pocket and read it as if checking

3

something. While he did that, I quickly unscrewed the cap, my hand trembling a little, and poured the sugar into the tank. I replaced the cap and we moved on.

Next it was Stefan's turn. It was a bit more nerve-racking to be the lookout. At least while you did the deed you were too busy concentrating on it to worry, but as I kept a lookout for Stefan I was painfully aware of just how many armed soldiers were roaming around. There were open trucks full of troops driving up and down, there were marching patrols with their machine guns at the ready, and there were soldiers moving everywhere. The city was theirs now, no longer ours. We managed to empty our pockets without any trouble though, and then we decided to hang around to see if it really worked.

A German officer stepped smartly out of a building, his driver just ahead of him. They got into one of the cars we'd sabotaged and tried to start the engine. It made a funny kind of noise and then just died. The driver got out, opened the hood, and spent ages trying to figure out the problem. Just behind him the same thing was happening with a large truck filled with soldiers waiting to be driven somewhere. Stefan and I had to lean against a building, we were laughing so hard. But it was dangerous to stick around. We got our bikes and headed home. "This is just the beginning, Jesper," Stefan howled in glee as we rode across the bridge to my apartment block.

"Just the beginning," I sang back, feeling elated beyond anything I had felt before. We weren't helpless, we weren't giving up without a fight. We'd show them!

We continued putting sugar in gas tanks at every opportunity, but after a couple of months we began to get bored. In June we had examinations and couldn't think about much else. Then came summer holidays. We had nothing to do but watch most of the Danish population try to pretend nothing was happening, and every day we got more and more angry and more and more restless. We went to Nelson Eddy and Jeanette MacDonald movies over and over again and we both wished we were Mounties with red uniforms and horses. And, of course, guns. *Guns*. What we could do with guns! We started to think about it and talk about it until we could think and talk about nothing else. We had to have guns. Well, at least one.

"Look," Stefan said to me one day, "if we can just get one, we can use it to hold up Germans

5

and get more, and then we can give them to our friends and we can start doing *real* raids. Like shooting up their headquarters, and stuff like that."

When I think back I realize how naive we were, but in our minds it was the sensible thing to do. After all, the city was full of weapons. All we had to do was outwit one dumb soldier and grab his gun. Maybe naive is a bit of an understatement. We made plans to meet that night on the steps of the school.

I'm an only child and my parents used to keep pretty close watch on me. They were good friends with Stefan's parents; in fact, Stefan's dad had operated on my dad when his appendix burst. They had developed a real rapport in the hospital and they had been friends ever since. All I had to do was say I was going to Stefan's. Stefan said he was going to my place.

"Have any trouble getting out?" I asked.

"Not from my parents," he said, and I could hear from his voice that he was still irritated, "but from my stupid sister. 'If Stefan can go out after supper, why can't I? I want to go to Susanne's.' Honestly!"

"So Lisa's a pain, so what? You're here."

I almost laugh thinking back to that remark. That "pain" grew up from a gawky, obnoxious kid into a beautiful, brave girl who forced her way into the resistance and . . . But I'm getting way ahead of myself. I said I was going to put this in order. That night Lisa was still just a pain, and the only thing on my mind was getting a gun.

We didn't actually have a plan. We decided we'd ride around the city, try to find a soldier who was alone and wasn't really paying attention, and then steal his gun. We headed downtown. The sky was clear blue that evening — the sun wouldn't set for hours — and I remember how beautiful the city looked as we drove over the bridge. Boats slid over the smooth surface of the lake, the trees by the shore were in full bloom, flowers created a riot of colour everywhere. Everything looked so peaceful and normal. Those damned Nazis had no right to be here! We decided to ride past the outdoor cafés. Perhaps a soldier would sling his rifle over a chair while relaxing, and one of us could create a diversion while the other got the gun.

Well, there were lots of German soldiers in the cafés — some of them sitting with Danish women, too, which really made me sick — but none of them was being careless with his gun that night. By ten-thirty it was late and we were tired, thirsty and discouraged. Neither of

7

us wanted to fail, to go home empty-handed, but it seemed we had no choice. I told Stefan I'd ride with him to the school, which was halfway between our two apartments. By the time we got there it was almost dark.

"Hey," Stefan whispered, putting a hand on my arm, catching me as I was about to ride off, "look."

I looked. Walking across the soccer field, rifle slung over his shoulder, was a German soldier. Alone.

"Leave your bike here," Stefan hissed. "Let's go!" We began to walk rapidly across the field.

"Maybe we should talk and laugh," I whispered. "Then he won't suspect anything."

"He doesn't suspect anything now," whispered Stefan. "He doesn't know we're here. Let's keep it that way."

It's funny to think back on it now. I wanted that gun so badly that I forgot to think about the possibility that I could be in any danger. Stefan and I grew closer and closer, until we were only ten steps behind him. Then Stefan gave me the nod. We were just about to spring ahead and grab the gun when the German whirled around and took a fighting stance, braced for attack. We were looking down the barrel of the rifle.

"What do you want?" he shouted. In German, of course.

I honestly think my heart ended up in my mouth, because I couldn't say a word.

Stefan kept his wits — thank God — because the soldier turned out to be a kid only a few years older than us. He was obviously scared stiff and ready to shoot us out of pure nervousness.

"Hey, we're just on our way home." Stefan smiled, and he spoke German too, which helped. "You've got the gun," he added. "We can't hurt you."

"Right!" the soldier yelled, embarrassed now because he'd shown his fear. "Get out of here. Fast! Move!"

We moved. We crossed the field, and when he was out of sight we circled back for our bikes. We were silent until we got to them, but then I began to get a funny feeling in my stomach. It quickly moved from my stomach up to my throat, where it became a snort, and the snort became a laugh, and soon I was howling, doubled over. I mean, it really did strike me as pretty funny, and besides, I guess I had some pent-up tension to get rid of. Stefan quickly caught the laugh and we rolled around on the school steps practically hysterical for a good five minutes. Whenever I tried to stop, Stefan would point at me and gasp, "The look on your face," and knowing what a terrified idiot I must have appeared, I'd start all over again.

We were both kept home for a week for getting back so late. A full week of summer holidays stuck in that apartment . . . I thought I'd go crazy. But it was right after that week that things began to get exciting, because I made contact with a real resistance organization.

2

It was Kurt, a cousin of mine, who confided to me that he and some friends were printing illegal newspapers. He told me how important these papers were in getting the real war news to the people and in convincing them to join resistance groups. He said he and his friends needed help distributing the papers, so I volunteered for both Stefan and me right then and there. That was our first real job. We'd pick a bag of papers up at a playground, then get on and off streetcars leaving copies. It was dangerous, but we thrived on it. We were sure we were much too smart to get caught. And we were lucky. Before long, Lisa started helping that way too. At first we didn't want her to. We thought she was too young — she wasn't even thirteen — and I guess we thought she wasn't brave enough. But she was incredibly stubborn, and we finally had to let her help.

After a couple of months of helping with the papers, Kurt put me in touch with a sabotage group. At first Stefan wasn't included, because he was Jewish, and if he were caught the Germans would use him as an example of what a dangerous threat the Jews were. The resistance didn't want to give the Germans any excuses for rounding up Jews. But Stefan insisted and I stuck by him and finally he was accepted as well.

The night we went on our first training mission was exciting beyond our wildest dreams. We sneaked out of our homes and were driven through the blacked-out city into the countryside. We were not only going to be given guns, we were going to learn how to use them! Mostly the resistance was using guns stolen from Germans. Others had obviously been more successful at that than we had been.

We drove deep into a forest outside Copenhagen and practised shooting for hours. It was December, I think; at any rate it was cold and damp. But that didn't bother Stefan and me. It was kind of difficult to practise shooting when it was pitch dark, but we didn't have much choice. We just had to be careful not to cut each other down. It was like a dream come true for me. Now I *was* Nelson Eddy. From then on I had my own machine gun, which I kept hidden under my mattress. It was a bit lumpy and uncomfortable, but if my parents had caught me with a gun . . . well, I hate to think. As it was, I'm sure they suspected what I was up to. I started to go out almost every night after supper. I suppose they realized I was getting too old to keep at home or discipline, and they probably just prayed I'd be all right.

We trained and we waited and finally one day we went on our first real mission.

The resistance was still small then and they were very anxious to do as much sabotage as possible, partly because they wanted to cripple the Germans in every way but also because of what had happened when the Germans invaded Denmark. Our government had surrendered to the Germans, but then it had stayed in power. Our king was still on the throne, and we weren't even at war with Germany; the Germans called us a "protectorate" — as if they were doing us a favour by protecting us. A lot of us hated this deal. The resistance had to remind everybody that the Germans were an invading enemy and that it was wrong to collaborate with them. Also, we hoped that as the sabotage got worse, the Nazis would get madder and make life in Denmark so horrible that the government would no longer be able to cooperate with them. Which is what finally happened in 1943. And if we didn't blow up places like armaments factories, the British would drop bombs on them, and lots of innocent Danish lives would be lost.

Our first mission was to blow up a factory that made fuselages and wings for German aircraft. It was all done in broad daylight. Stefan and I met our two contacts at Olaf's garage at exactly one p.m. Twenty minutes later we were standing with them at one end of the street while four others stood at the far end. It was our job to stop traffic. I was pretty disappointed. I guess I'd been hoping to run around and do some shooting. Instead we were just very polite and told people that there was trouble down the street and they'd have to wait. If anyone had made trouble we'd have shown them our guns, but nobody did. Ten minutes later there was a huge explosion. We jumped in our cars and took off down a side street, and that was that. Easy.

The raids were always planned out to the last detail, leaving nothing to chance. Stefan and I had only one person as a contact. It was safer that way; if we were caught and tortured we couldn't betray the rest of the group. I know all about that now. There's another rule, too. Hold out under torture for twenty-four hours; that'll give your contacts a chance to go underground. Then talk if you have to.

Soon after that first action, we raided a Danish police headquarters and stole all their guns. They didn't put up too much of a fight. I'm sure a lot of them hated doing the Germans' dirty work. In fact, we got most of our drawings of the factories we were blowing up from the police. As soon as the sabotage actions began, the Germans had demanded protection from the Danish police. The Danes replied that in order to protect the Germans they would need lists of all the factories, and detailed floor plans too, so they could place their men properly. These lists and floor plans mysteriously made their way directly to the underground and we used them to plan our raids. We always knew how many guards there were, where they were stationed, where the machinery was — and the Germans could never figure out how we did it.

Stefan and I led pretty happy lives for those few years, until the fall of 1943. We went to school, kept up our studies, and got more and more active in sabotage. We were never close to getting caught. We often went to mass demonstrations where people would gather to sing. Thousands would crowd into the town hall square and sing Danish songs. It wasn't illegal, the Germans couldn't stop us, but they hated every moment. And once I remember the king shook my hand. He used to ride through the streets on his horse every morning, greeting his citizens, cheering us, trying to give us hope.

Also, by then I was dating Lisa. Although she was only fifteen, Lisa got more and more involved in the resistance. Soon she and her best friend Susanne joined our sabotage group. Lisa and I would go to a movie in the afternoon and a sabotage action after dinner. By that time there were six or seven sabotage acts every day, so the Germans put troops in to guard the factories. When people went to work and saw German troops they got so mad that they started to demonstrate and riot. Then the Germans started taking hostages, and that caused more riots. So the Germans demanded that the Danes themselves crack down on their people by shooting them. The Danish government refused, and on August 29 it ceased to exist. Now, finally, the whole country was together, at war. Olaf, who was still our main resistance contact, invited Stefan and me to share a bottle of whisky with him — something he'd swiped in a raid — and we all got drunk that night as we celebrated. I suffered the next day. I threw up all day and my mother almost took me to the hospital; she was sure I had some horrible flu. But my father took one look at my colour and told her I'd be fine. I thought I'd probably die; I even sort of wished I would. I don't think I'll ever drink whisky again. Not that I suppose I'll have the chance.

And then I lost Stefan and Lisa, and everything changed, and suddenly it wasn't a game any more. Until then the Jews had been treated exactly the same as everyone else. When the Nazis wanted the Jews to wear yellow stars on their coats, the king replied that if one of his citizens had to wear a star, all his citizens, including him, would wear them. I guess the prospect of the entire population wearing stars was enough to finish *that* idea. But we read about the concentration camps in the resistance newspapers and heard about the mass murders of Jews in other occupied countries. Then in October the Germans decided to round up the Jews in Denmark, too. They'd been afraid to do it before that because they knew the Danes would turn against them — but now that the Danes had turned against them anyway, they must have figured they had nothing to lose. They planned to capture all the Jewish families in their homes on Rosh Hashanah, the Jewish New Year.

That night Stefan and Lisa hid at the hospital where their dad was a surgeon. Other Jewish families went to friends, neighbours, churches or hospitals, and when the Germans came to get them no one was home. The resistance swung into frantic action. We had to find a way to smuggle all these families across the sound to Sweden. I didn't sleep at all those first few nights; there just wasn't time. I lost touch with Lisa and Stefan until the night they were smuggled out of the hospital to the coast. I met up with them there and the three of us helped the groups coming from Copenhagen get onto boats for Sweden. Finally it was their turn to go. I kissed Lisa as she left, our first real kiss, and then I stood there on the beach, alone, my best friend and his sister disappearing into the darkness. Gunfire exploded around me and I found myself in the middle of a German raid on the beach. The black moonless night saved me and I managed to escape.

After that I sort of stopped going to school for

the month of October. I worked day and night helping to smuggle out the rest of the Jews, who were hidden in hospitals or churches or — one of our favourite spots — a bookstore right opposite Gestapo headquarters. Out of seven thousand Jews, the Germans caught only about four hundred.

I have to walk up and down. I'm so cold, and my feet are numb. But when I move I get a horrible stabbing pain in my fingers, as if they're being attacked with little sharp knives. I look down at them. Some are more swollen than others. There's pus oozing out of the ripped flesh of the baby finger. I think of my mother's hands — always smooth and cool and soothing, caressing my hot forehead when I was sick, or impossibly fast and nimble when she did her sewing. She was sewing the night I went to Olaf's garage, the night I met Frederik again.

It was a cold, rainy night in November and, as usual, I was listening to the BBC on the radio after dinner. It was illegal but everyone did it. It told us what was really happening in the war, and it was also the way the resistance got important coded messages from England. My father was out of town on a sales trip, and my mother was sitting sewing a Pierrot costume for a pantomime at the Tivoli amusement park.

My mind wandered away from the news and drifted into daydreams about Tivoli, with its rides, restaurants and outdoor stages all built around beautiful little lakes. I remembered sitting on a restaurant patio there with Lisa, looking over the water, under the shade of thick old trees. At night the whole park is lit up with thousands of lights and looks like every child's dream of fairyland. I love it there.

My mother was an actress before she married and had me, and then she started sewing costumes for the pantomime. She was allowed to watch rehearsals, and of course she took me along, so Tivoli became my second home. The people there got to know me so well that they offered to let me go on the rides for free. At first I wouldn't go on any. I was too scared. So one day my father came to Tivoli with us and he picked me up and carried me onto the roller coaster. I thought I'd die of fear. It's an amazing roller coaster, huge and high and fast, and I was too petrified even to scream. When it was over and my white knuckles were still gripping the bar so hard I couldn't let go, my father said to me, "Are you dead or alive?"

"Alive," I whispered, my voice cracking.

"Good," he replied. "Then we'll go again."

And we did, until I wasn't afraid any more.

"You see," he said, "if you die you have nothing to worry about, and if you don't there's no point making yourself sick worrying about dying."

Suddenly I heard the word "Peter" breaking into my daydreams.

"What was that?" I asked my mother, praying she'd been listening to the broadcast.

"Oh, nothing," she replied. "Just birthday greetings and best wishes to Peter and Robert and some others."

My stomach gave a small lurch. Peter — that was the code name for our cell. It meant there was to be a drop of weapons tonight. I'd have to meet the group at Olaf's garage. I grabbed my jacket, gave my mom a kiss, and said I'd be back later. I knew she hated my going out like that, but I was seventeen and she knew she couldn't stop me.

When I got to the garage Olaf and John were waiting for me. John was in his early twenties, a medical student.

"Who else?" I asked. I knew there must be more than three; we needed at least four people to shine lights to mark the place where the British plane was to make the drop.

"Lars should be here any minute," Olaf responded. I didn't know Lars and I wasn't sure if that was his code name or his real name. Naturally, I didn't ask.

In a couple of minutes Lars showed up. He was a big man, like Olaf, which was good because those containers could be miserably heavy.

We climbed into Olaf's truck, Lars and I riding in the open back and Olaf driving. Something in the BBC message would have confirmed the drop site — probably the best wishes bit — but only Olaf knew that part of the code. We headed out of Copenhagen toward Roskilde. The country road was pitch black, no lights anywhere.

After about a half-hour drive we slowed down and Olaf turned off into a farmer's field. We got out, each of us running to a corner of the field. Then we waited. I stood under a group of trees to get what protection I could. It was cold out there, and the wind blew right through my jacket. At least it had stopped raining. Clouds scudded by overhead and a half moon shed a weak light on the countryside.

My Sten gun was slung over my shoulder on a strap. Now, the thing about those Sten guns is that it takes nothing, and I mean nothing, for the safety to slip off, and then, if the gun is loaded, it can blast away until the entire magazine is empty. And when I say it was cold, I mean *cold*. I didn't have a windproof jacket because they were almost impossible to get and so, well, I started to shiver. I guess I shivered so badly that the strap slipped, because the gun slammed to the ground and started firing, propelling itself around on the ground in a quick, jerky circle. Thank God for all the exercising I'd done! I jumped as high as I could, grabbed a branch, and hung there helplessly, my knees bent into my body, desperately trying not to get shot by my own gun. The others ran over very cautiously — and scared stiff — thinking I'd encountered a German patrol. They got there just as the magazine emptied. I jumped down, but not before they'd seen me. Olaf and John almost fell over, they laughed so hard. Lars just glared at me. Guess I'd really scared him. I knew I'd never live that one down — I could hear the jokes already.

Then dimly, through the laughter, we heard a sound, an airplane. We all raced back to our positions. Lars was the first to put on his flashlight. Normally we'd wait until we could hear the engines clearly, to make sure it was a British plane and not a German one. We could all tell the difference by then. But I thought

Lars must have his reasons for putting on his light, so I did the same, and so did Olaf and John. Now flashlights beamed through the darkness from all four corners of the field. The plane would drop its cargo right in the centre, where the four beams met.

But the more I listened, the less I liked the sound of that plane. It sounded . . . sounded like . . . yes, I was sure. Quickly I snapped off my light. So did Olaf and John. Finally Lars did, but too late. It was a German patrol plane and it roared right overhead. I was sure it had seen the lights. Now what to do? They'd come back and strafe us — or, if they were on their way somewhere more important, they'd radio ground patrols to come out and get us. But there was an English plane coming, and we couldn't leave till we'd had our rendezvous with it.

Again, silence. As I waited in the dark, I started to worry about Lars. What a stupid mistake! But perhaps he was new and very green. The German plane didn't return, and finally, after what seemed like years, I heard engines again. We all waited until we'd heard them properly — yes, it was a British plane. All our lights went on practically simultaneously. The plane dove in low over us and we saw two parachutes open and fall to the ground. Lights off, we scrambled into the centre of the field and ripped the parachute lines off the containers. There were four of them, two attached to each parachute. We left the chutes for the moment and began lugging the containers to the truck, which was parked near the road. We heaved two of the containers into the truck. Suddenly Olaf hissed:

"Look!"

At least four sets of headlights were moving toward us.

"Into the truck," he ordered. He jumped into the driver's seat and we leaped into the back. Headlights off, he drove into the field and stopped near the containers. German patrol or no German patrol, we couldn't afford to leave those weapons behind. He scrambled out to help us and somehow we got them into the truck and hopped in beside them. Olaf drove away through the field, with the rest of us crouched among the containers, ready to shoot. I was pretty worried since I had no more ammunition.

The Germans followed us across the field and started to fire, but they were still too far away to hit us.

Olaf reached a small dirt road and raced

down it. It twisted and turned in among the trees and I was sure the Germans couldn't see us any more. Of course, they had the advantage of having their headlights on, and their trucks were faster. But Olaf headed across another field. He had lived in Roskilde and knew the area like the back of his hand. On the far side of the field we started down a tree-lined road in the opposite direction, backtracking in the hope that the Germans would chase off in the wrong direction. Quickly Olaf veered off the road into another field. It occurred to me that he'd better be careful or we'd all end up in a ditch somewhere.

Thump.

Somehow I was convinced, at that moment, that it was my thought that had made it happen. I was practically jolted out of the truck, and when I looked around I saw that we were indeed in a ditch. We all leaped out and tried to push but it was hopeless; the ditch was too deep.

I could see a light in a farmhouse a short distance away.

"Let's go," Olaf whispered. "We'll get help there."

I ran to the door and knocked. A middle-aged man answered, still in his overalls, a smoking pipe in his hand.

I smiled. "Hi! I'm awfully sorry to bother you, sir," I said, trying to look as sheepish as possible, "but, well, you see, my girlfriend and I came out here for, well, a little privacy, and, well, we're sort of lost, could you just show us . . ."

Obligingly the farmer stepped out onto the porch.

Olaf stuck a gun in his back. "Sorry, sir," he said, "no time to find out if you're a good Dane or not. We just need some help. Get your horses ready. We need them to pull our truck out of the ditch."

The poor farmer dropped his pipe.

He led us to the barn and with shaky hands he prepared the horses. Lars helped him; he'd obviously been brought up on a farm. They led the horses through the dark to the truck and hitched them up, and the horses started to pull. Slowly, slowly, they strained, and finally the truck jolted up and out of the ditch onto solid ground. Unfortunately, we'd all been so worried about being stuck that none of us had had the presence of mind to close up the back of the truck, and as it tilted up on its way out of the ditch, all the containers slid out and crashed to the ground.

Olaf threw up his hands in frustration.

"Lars, you and I will get these back in the truck," he said. "Meantime you two" — he pointed to me and John — "take this good man back home and tie him up and put him in with his horses. Can't afford to have him calling in our whereabouts to the Germans."

"No, no, I won't," the farmer protested, but John and I led him and his horses back to the barn, and we tied him up next to one of the horses for warmth. I felt bad doing it, but that was the horrible thing — you *never* knew who could be trusted, and we couldn't endanger our group just to be kind and polite to an old farmer.

By the time we got back to the truck it was loaded up and ready to go. Olaf drove up and down the country roads for another hour, but we seemed to have lost the patrol. We covered the containers with a tarpaulin and drove to the outskirts of Copenhagen, to an old deserted warehouse. Within minutes the truck was unloaded and we were heading back to the garage. Olaf opened the garage door and we drove in. I sighed and smiled and opened my mouth to speak — when suddenly all the lights flashed on and we were surrounded by soldiers. There were guns everywhere. For a split second I couldn't understand it. It was too much of a shock. All I could think was, *How? Who?*

Then I remembered how Lars had turned his light on for the German plane. I looked at him. He didn't seem surprised. I wanted to kill him. I grabbed for my gun and remembered that it was empty. My stomach turned over: I hadn't felt so sick since that day on the roller coaster. I reached for the cyanide capsule that was always in my pocket, but too late. My whole body was slammed into the truck, my arms pinned behind me. Damn. Damn. *Damn!*

3

They had my gun. Evidence. My hands were
cuffed roughly behind my back and I was
dragged outside and thrown into a black Opel
Kapitan that roared up in front of the garage.
I tried to turn my head to see what was happening to the others but one of my two escorts
whacked me across the back of the neck. I tried
to hit him back but, of course, I was helpless.
Yes, helpless. And scared. For the first time.
How odd. I'd never even thought about getting
caught; it had never really entered my head.
All the narrow escapes had been sort of like a
game that I was bound to win. It registered
somewhere in my brain that I was sweating,
even though I was freezing cold, and that my
teeth wanted to chatter. I couldn't let them: I
couldn't let the Nazis see my fear, or they'd use

it. And my feeling of being helpless — they'd use that, too. My cyanide pill was still inside my shirt pocket, and I had to decide whether to take it. Would I even get the chance? I decided against it, hoping I could hold out for twenty-four hours. I didn't know too many names, and I could keep giving them the names of the men they'd caught with me. They'd find those out quickly enough anyway. I'd say they were my only contacts. I felt thankful that I knew only their code names.

Suddenly — with a shock, as if someone had punched me — I thought of my mother and our little apartment, and of how at breakfast tomorrow they'd know something had happened. It would break their hearts — I was all they had. My mother would worry herself to death. How can you do this to them, I thought, instantly hating myself. Then I thought of school and how I'd be sure to fall behind in my studies. I almost laughed aloud. Get behind in my studies? Yes, I guessed I would. And there was an English literature class the next day that I'd especially wanted to be at. My eyes were full of tears but I wouldn't cry, I couldn't let them see me cry. I had to calm down, be in control. They'd be a lot older than me, my interrogators, and a lot meaner. I thought of

Tivoli and the roller coaster and my fear, and I said to myself, "You'll either die or you won't, but the fear is useless." It worked. The fear left me and I took a long, slow, calming breath.

"Heraus! Schnell!" they shouted at me as the car stopped.

Oh, how I hate the German language! I hate the sound of it. Especially those words, *"Heraus,"* *"Schnell."* I've been hearing them since the Germans first got here. I remember the second day after they'd invaded Copenhagen. I was walking along the street after supper to go to see Stefan, and these soldiers were walking behind me. I wasn't moving fast enough for their liking and one of them kicked me in the behind, really hard, and yelled *"Schnell, schnell!"* I vowed then and there that I'd move, but never the way they told me to.

I looked around to see where the car had stopped. I wouldn't move fast enough so they pushed me out. My heart sank. We were at Dagmarhus, the Gestapo headquarters. Each soldier took one of my arms and together they pulled me along into the building, up two flights of steps, into a small office.

A Gestapo officer sat behind a desk. He didn't even look up when I was brought in, but continued with his paperwork. The guards shoved me down into a chair.

"Name," he barked.

"Kris," I responded, giving my code name. I was shaken so my voice came out in a kind of hoarse whisper, making me sound frightened.

"Oh," he laughed, still not looking up, "we have a little Kris mouse here."

The guards roared with laughter at his pathetic joke and finally he looked up. For a brief second I was sure I knew him; he seemed terribly familiar in some way. He was young, perhaps mid-twenties, and good looking. He stared at me, his blue eyes hard and cold, but with a fixed intensity, as if he might know me too.

"Your real name, please."

"Kris," I replied, more firmly.

He made a motion with his hand. One of the guards slapped me hard across the face with the back of his glove. I could feel my lip and cheek open and start to bleed. It hurt — a lot — and my eyes stung. I could feel fear rising in me, but then other emotions took over. Blind rage and hatred. And yet, through it all, the Gestapo man looked so familiar. At the back of my mind a voice kept nagging at me that I knew him.

Just then the phone rang. He answered, listened, put it down.

"Take him to Vestre Jail," he said to the guards.

The guards pulled me to my feet and dragged me out of the office, down the stairs, and back into the Opel. I was then driven across the city into the west end to the Vestre Jail. I'd driven past it with my parents at various times and had always rather admired the rounded-out door built into the outer wall, with its triangular redbrick decorations. It didn't look quite so pretty or quaint close up. It was a huge jail built in the shape of a cross, and once past the outer wall I saw why it had a reputation for ugliness as well as size. Great iron bars clanged behind me and I was dragged through the inner door, down hallways filled with prisoners, and into an empty cell. Then they searched me, removed my belt, untied my hands, and left me. I immediately felt inside my shirt pocket to see if they'd found the cyanide pill. They had, and it was gone.

I sat on the iron cot and tried to think, tried to sort out what had just happened. And then it hit me. Like bomb. That Gestapo officer looked just like Frederik. Was it possible? Why hadn't I recognized him immediately? Why didn't *he* recognize *me*? Well, I'd last seen him before the war. He'd changed, grown into man. And of course he wouldn't recognize me. I'd been a kid when I'd last seen him.

Frederik . . . in a Nazi uniform? I didn't want to believe it. Maybe it was just someone who looked like him. I sat in the cell and forgot about my surroundings, my predicament, everything, as I remembered that first day when I met Frederik.

I was about ten years old — well, no, I was ten and a half, almost eleven, because it was September. It was my first beach party. Our whole class went to the beach in Amager, an island attached by a bridge to Copenhagen, and Frederik came along as a chaperone. Rosa, his younger sister, was in my class. I remember she had yellow braids and rosy cheeks and was quite plump, and whenever she looked at me she blushed and giggled. I guess she had a crush on me. Well, Rosa may have had a crush on me but I had a crush on Helen. Helen was new to our school. She'd come from Hirtshals in the north of Denmark. She was tall, with silky brown hair and big brown eyes, and she never smiled. I admired that it always looked as if she had a secret she wouldn't share with us — and also the fact that she was a bit aloof and definitely cleverer than all of us put together. Her grades weren't actually that good — not as good as mine (I was always top of the class) — but I thought that was because she was new.

I was determined to impress her, anyway. I was tall for my age and in good shape because I played soccer every day. I decided I'd swim out to a boat moored in the harbour and suddenly appear on deck waving at everyone. When I think about it now it doesn't seem like such a great feat, but it did then. It seemed like a very impressive thing to do. Anyway, I swam out, but the weather was grey and the wind was blowing and the waves were pretty high. As I swam the boat seemed to get farther and farther away, and I realized that all I was doing was fighting the waves. As I turned back, exhausted, a wave washed over me and I got a mouthful of salt water. Then I really started to worry that I would go down. I yelled for help, forgetting all pride and about making a good impression. I started to swim for my life, but my arms and legs felt like lead and I kept choking. I figured I'd had it, when a pair of strong arms lifted me and towed me back into shallow water. I managed to stagger to shore on my own and that's when I met Frederik, my rescuer. Although in a way I almost wished he'd let me drown, I was so humiliated. Rosa stopped giggling long enough to cry, but Helen's expression didn't change. I discovered later that it never did — she wasn't really cool and aloof. She was grumpy and sour and she never smiled because she was never happy.

Anyway, there was Frederik. Tall, muscular, thick blond hair, tanned skin, eyes the same blue as the ocean on a day when it glitters in the sun — the kind of guy you *knew* would always get any girl he wanted. He slapped me on the back — which in my weakened state almost knocked me over — and shook my hand and almost crushed it. Then he said I should come over to his house after the party. He'd show me how to workout so I could build up my muscles. Soccer gives you good endurance, of course, and my legs were strong, but if could look like that . . . ! So I went, and Rosa seemed pretty pleased, and Frederik showed me lots of exercises and said I could come and workout with him once a week — if I wanted to. If I wanted to! I was sick of being the "brain" of the class. I mean, brains are okay, but I wanted to be just like him.

We kept it up for about a year. We added chess to our weekly meetings, too. And he could beat me. He was the only person I knew who could beat me — including my own parents and all my classmates. He became like an older brother to me, and for an only child that was awfully important. He was always kind to me, too. Of course, sometimes he would kid me and tease me — especially about Rosa — just the way an older brother should. He'd tell me to get my nose out of my books and ask his sister out before she pined away from love. I was too young to date, but I did take her for an ice cream once, and all she did was giggle the entire time; I don't think she uttered one word. He teased me even more after that, but never in front of Rosa. He never made either of us feel stupid or anything. Now that I think back, I realize that we didn't talk much — but we were very comfortable with each other.

Also, I think in some ways we were very much alike. I couldn't help but wonder why he'd waste his Sunday afternoons on an eleven-year-old kid when he could be dating girls or out with the boys. I remember him telling me, in a rare burst of confidentiality, that he felt painfully ill at ease in groups. He muttered something about his father being so strict he'd never had a chance to be with other kids, or even to relax in his own house — and

I could see that was true. I was terrified of his father, who was a real tyrant. Well, the funny thing was that although my parents were the exact opposite — never strict, always encouraging me to go out with friends — I was also shy and self-conscious. I was always kidded about being "the brain," just as he was, and I *never* seemed to know what to say.

I guess I was almost twelve when I last saw him — in the autumn of 1938. He'd decided to go to Germany to study German language and literature. I missed him terribly. He warned me he hated to write and he was true to his word, but Rosa sent me greetings from him every now and then.

Was it possible? Could it be Frederik? Maybe it was and he was in deep cover, a double agent working for the Danish resistance. Yes, I thought, maybe that was it! He was one of us and he was doing an incredibly dangerous job, and even if he did recognize me he couldn't show it. I'd have to . . .

My cell door slammed open.

"This way," a soldier ordered. "Looks like your luck has just run out. You're taking a little trip to Ryvangen."

I tried to keep my face from showing anything. "Oh," I said lightly, "is it a nice night for a ride?"

I was handcuffed and taken out into the dark and lifted up into an open truck. There were eight of us in the truck, four to a bench, and three soldiers. The truck lurched forward and, as we moved through the blacked-out streets of our city, the man beside me started to whistle. He was whistling the Danish national anthem. I joined in. Soon there was quite a chorus going.

"Shut up," shouted the soldiers, and they began to go around slapping everyone on the face and head. I got jabbed in the stomach with a rifle butt. The pain was excruciating and I doubled over with a groan, the wind completely knocked out of me.

"That should keep you quiet," the soldier muttered. One by one the others stopped whistling.

"Ryvangen," laughed a German. "Whistle all you want there."

I'm sure everyone in the truck knew about Ryvangen. It's an old Danish army barracks in the north of Copenhagen, with a park for parade attached to it. Now the park has become the Gestapo's execution grounds. It was funny, though: I wasn't scared. I felt quite peaceful. Perhaps it was because I wasn't alone. The person beside me started to whistle again — very quietly.

4

As we drove on through the city, I suppose my strongest emotion was sadness — the kind of deep regret you feel when saying goodbye to those you love; not only the people you love but the places, too. Copenhagen was my home. The city was full of memories. It was dark, I couldn't see much, but I could tell approximately where we were going. We drove away from downtown and the shops, and the outdoor restaurant where my parents used to take me on sunny Saturday afternoons, where we'd listen to jazz and they'd drink beer; away from the streets where my friends and I used to walk up and down hoping to bump into girls we liked; into the residential areas of the northern part of the city, past the huge parks, the statues, the houses with their copper roofs turned green with age, the apartment buildings built in the late twenties. I could smell the ocean; the wind was damp, as always, with seawater.

We arrived at Ryvangen and the truck shuddered to a halt. I thought of my family, of Lisa, of Stefan. I hoped they all knew how much I cared for them.

"Heraus! Schnell, schnell!" Were those the last words I was to hear before I died? The soldiers used their rifle butts to shove us out of the truck into a central courtyard with barracks all around and lights shining down from above. We were called by name or by number — I suppose those prisoners who wouldn't even reveal their code names had been given numbers. When we'd been identified we were marched off in two groups of four, again pushed ahead by rifle butts. We were marched past a barracks house, then down a cobblestone path into a boulevard of trees. At this point our two groups split away from each other.

My group was herded off the main path onto a narrow one surrounded by trees. We were pushed deeper and deeper into the woods until we reached a small clearing, open on the side of the path but with banks of earth built up on the other sides. Four wooden poles were stuck in the ground in front of the far rise. One by one we were lashed to these poles. They didn't bother to uncuff my hands; they just tied me to the pole by winding the rope around my chest and my legs. Then five soldiers lined up in front of us, machine guns ready. I remember thinking what a beautiful night it was. The trees rose all around us, but when I looked straight up I could see stars. The branches made a beautiful sound as they rustled and swayed in the wind. I couldn't help but think what a peaceful spot this was.

One of the soldiers started to call out: "Ready, aim." I took a deep breath, said a prayer to God to protect those I loved, shut my eyes, held my breath, felt my heart hammering against my chest. No wonder they tied you up. My knees buckled, and I would have dropped to the ground.

"Fire."

The guns burst into an explosion of noise. It was odd, but I couldn't feel anything. Nothing. I had thought it would hurt. And . . . I could still hear. I heard laughter. I opened my eyes. The guards were laughing. They were roaring with laughter. For a moment I was terribly confused. Were the others dead? I couldn't tell.

Maybe the soldiers didn't realize they'd missed me. But they sauntered over to us and one by one each prisoner was untied. We were pushed down the paths back to the courtyard and then back into the truck. It had all been a fake, then. A fake. Once again we were seated, and the truck moved away from the field, the Germans still laughing. I guess at some point I had cried because my face was wet with tears. Then I noticed that there were only four of us in the truck. For the others it had not been a hoax but all too real.

The prisoner beside me muttered, "Just another of their favourite forms of torture. Now we'll be interrogated. More likely to talk now, don't you think?" There was an acrid smell in the truck, the fear and sweat of what everyone had just been through. I took a deep breath and the cold air bit into me, confirming that I was still alive.

The three Germans riding in the back with us stood up and started to sing a song, "*Muss Ich Denn,*" a sentimental piece they love to sing when they're swilling beer. I guess this had been terrific entertainment for them. They swayed back and forth belting out the words. But then one of them stopped and fell over, blood gushing from his head onto the prisoner beside me. The others stopped and looked around in surprise. They'd been singing so loudly that the shots had barely been audible. But we all heard them once the singing stopped.

I felt a surge of energy and hope rush through me. The truck careered around the street and I realized that the driver must have been shot, too. I threw myself onto the floor of the truck, as did the other prisoners, while the guards fired wildly with their machine guns. Another one got hit. He screamed in pain, and as he screamed, the truck reeled off the road and crashed headlong into a building. There was a severe jolt and my head thudded against the floor of the truck. The other German had been thrown down by the impact. All four of us rushed to sit on him to keep him from getting his machine gun and wiping us out. Someone cracked him over the head, hard, with his handcuffs and he passed out.

We scrambled off the truck. Two men stood in the street, guns at the ready. "This way," they whispered. "There are cars waiting for you." They ran down the street with us. Parked at its end was an ambulance. We jumped in, the two men slammed the doors behind us, and the ambulance took off as we hurled ourselves onto the cots, panting, still handcuffed.

"What about these?" I gasped, wanting the cuffs off more than anything, wanting not to feel helpless any more.

"I guess we're stuck with them until we get where we're going," said one of my companions. It was too dark to really see whom I was travelling with.

"Where do you think we're going?" I asked, more than a little puzzled. "And," I added, "couldn't they have done this on our way *there*, not on our way *back*? How'd they know it wouldn't just be a bunch of bodies? Those others," I added bitterly, "didn't make it."

"We have a man in Vestre Jail," answered someone in a deep, rough voice. "He'd have got word out to the resistance. But, you know, the Germans usually do these executions during the day, so the public can see them; it makes good fear propaganda for the Nazis. In this case, for whatever reason, they went for the night and it probably took our people a while to get organized and get out there. Just guessing, of course. But maybe they couldn't get there any faster."

"Do you know where we're going now?" I said.

"A safe house," was the answer. "Let's wait and see.

46

I was starting to be able to see my companions more clearly. I looked out the back window of the ambulance. The sky was no longer pitch black; it must have been very early morning. Quite a night, I thought. Quite a night.

My companions were all older than I was. One looked about fifty, with grey hair and a big potbelly; another was a man in his thirties; the other looked, well, pretty. Then I realized that it wasn't a man at all, but a woman dressed as a man, her hair tucked into her cap. She winked at me. I guess I'd been staring at her. My face burned and I felt like a real idiot.

The ambulance slowed down, then stopped. We stumbled out into the faint dawn and were hurried through the back door of a house. I could tell we were in a Copenhagen suburb, but not which one. A man in his thirties, with blond hair, met us and took us down to the basement. There, alongside a huge printing press and a table full of papers and materials, was a table with various tools. He motioned us over to it and picked up a small saw.

"Who's first?" he grinned.

We all deferred to the man with grey hair, who seemed to have a natural authority.

"Code names only," he commanded. Then, as

he placed his hands on the table, he introduced himself. "Needle," he said.

I tried not to show my surprise. He was — still is — a famous, influential resistance fighter. If the Germans only knew whom they let get away! And no wonder the resistance made such an effort to rescue us. The Needle knew too much. Better he and the rest of us die in an escape attempt than have the Germans get their hands on him.

"Henrik," said the other man.

"Janicke," said the young woman.

I smiled. "Kris," I said.

As he worked on cutting our handcuffs off, the young blond man introduced himself. "My name is Sven," he said, "and you'll be my guests for a while. Actually, it's quite handy to have you all here, as we can use some help on our press."

I looked around and then asked the question I felt I must ask — even though I already knew the answer. After all, I had recognized Frederik. He might have remembered me, too.

"I don't know if I should go home," I admitted. "The man who interrogated me may have recognized me. I don't know what to do."

The Needle looked at me and answered curtly, "Go underground. If he recognized you,

you and your family will be in danger. Don't contact your family in case they are being watched. Wait. Maybe after a while you can go back, see if it's safe. But best not to take chances."

I knew he was right, but I wished there were something I could do. I had never meant to put my family in danger. And I felt so cut off. I couldn't go home, I couldn't even let them know I was alive. And what if Frederik hadn't recognized me at all? I'd be underground for nothing. But if he had, he would wait patiently for me to turn up at home.

Unless he was a double agent working for the resistance — but if he was, no one would tell me, of course.

It appeared that I had no choice. I couldn't risk being caught again or putting my parents at risk. I would have to disappear and go underground.

I tried not to show my sense of loss, of isolation. Or my feelings of terrible frustration. My whole life would be different from that moment on, and yet this change was based not on fact but on uncertainty. Ever since the Germans took over, that has been at the forefront of all our lives — uncertainty. Nothing is sure. Nothing is safe. Is your neighbour a friend or an enemy? Before the war we could look our fellow Danes in the eye. Now we don't know if we are looking at a friend or an enemy.

5

Boots tramp along the corridor and I hear cell doors open, then slam shut again. It must be lunchtime. I shuffle over to the little wooden shelf built into the wall, where my metal tray is. How can I pick it up? My fingers won't work at all and even the slightest effort turns the pain from excruciating to unbearable. But I know I have to eat, to keep my strength up. On the other hand, if I'm to die anyway, why bother? I suppose trying to survive has become a habit. I cup the sides of the tray in the palms of my hands so I needn't use my fingers and I carry it over to the cell door. The door is opened. Two guards stand in front of it. One keeps his gun pointed directly at me while the other dishes out soup from a bucket. The cell door slams shut.

I get a bowl full of weak soup with half a potato floating in it, and a hunk of bread. They've thrown the bread in the soup, which is fine because it's too stale for me to break with my fingers or my teeth. I sit and try to eat. The soup is basically warm water.

I'm in a cell at the very top of Shellhuset, which has been the Gestapo headquarters since Dagmarhus got too small for them. It's also a jail for very important prisoners, leaders of the resistance. They put the cells up here in the attic of the building so the Allies won't bomb it. We're the hostages protecting all those Gestapo files and all those Gestapo officers. I suppose I'll be moved soon — or shot. I'm not important enough to keep here. In fact, I can't figure out why they've left me here so long already.

I'd better get back to my "story." When I let my mind wander I just end up thinking about when the guards will come for me next and what new torture they'll put me through. I have to act like a good news reporter — sort through the facts, pick and choose what's important, put things in order.

I put the tray back on the shelf and lie down on the bed, wrapping myself in the blanket. All right, where was I? Oh yes, I was underground in Copenhagen. Once I went into hiding I stayed with Sven and worked almost exclusively on the underground newspaper. When I was fourteen I thought that would be boring work, not half as exciting or important as sabotage, but I had seen over the years just how necessary it was. The underground press was what brought most of the Danes over to our side. At first many people believed the Nazi propaganda; some thought the Nazis weren't all that bad, and of course the news broadcasts kept saying the Germans were going to win the war, so a lot of people thought resistance was useless. But when they heard about the terrible things the Nazis were doing, and about the battles the Allies were winning, they began to change their minds. For instance, when the underground press reported the Allied landing in Italy there was a rush of new recruits who wanted to join the resistance. Most people became more and more willing to fight the Germans and less and less willing to collaborate. I had always loved the written word — literature was my favourite subject — but now I saw what real power it could have.

Many of the people working on the underground press were reporters. Some still worked on the official papers, others had gone underground, like me. And they taught me. I learned to type. I learned how to run the press and even how to fix it if it broke. Also, I went out to cover stories. We had a big advantage over the official papers: we got to hear about the stories even before they happened. We'd get a call telling us there was going to be a sabotage action and we'd go out, take pictures, write up the story and have it to our subscribers the next morning.

At first Sven edited everything I wrote, rewriting a lot of it, but as I gained experience he began to leave me alone, only changing stories occasionally. I was always happy for his advice — he was a real pro. Janicke turned out to be a trained photographer, so we went out on the stories together. She was two years older than me. She'd been a university student until the Germans caught her photographing their installations along the coast. Henrik and the Needle moved on. The Needle was in constant touch with the Freedom Council, seven resistance fighters who directed all underground activities and, in the absence of any Danish government, spoke to the Germans on behalf of the Danish people. Only through messages, of course. If the Germans caught one of the Freedom Council he'd be worth his weight in gold. The resistance had become tightly organized by then, and very well coordinated.

At any rate, the month of June 1944 sticks out in my mind — well, that whole summer, really. It was an amazing summer, both wonderful and horrible. I'd been underground, let's see, eight months by then. We'd had to move the press three times; the Germans had been right on our heels each time. We'd ended up in a small house that Sven owned on Amager. Amager is part of the city of Copenhagen, but it's a separate island; large bridges connect it to the rest of the city. I used to go out at night to cover the stories, then spend the days writing them up, although sometimes that was reversed. Some actions took place in broad daylight, especially the railway sabotage. I was beginning to think that if the war ever ended I might like to be a journalist. I was certainly getting good training.

The most incredible moment of all those eight months came on June 6, when we listened to the BBC and heard that the Allies had managed to land on the French coast, in Normandy. We all cheered and clapped, hugged and shook hands. I'll never forget that broadcast. General Eisenhower spoke to us and I felt he was talking directly to me. "The hour of your liberation is approaching," he said. "And to members of resistance movements, follow your instructions." I think those were his words — but I'm sure about "The hour of your liberation is approaching." Every night before I went to sleep I would repeat those words over and over, and I could hear his voice as it had come through the crackle and buzz of the radio set. Soon we'd have Denmark back. Soon we'd be free.

That month resistance activity skyrocketed. There were major sabotage actions every day, and the Germans got madder and madder. I think they were beginning to sense that they were losing control.

On June 22 the resistance blew up a gun factory right here in Copenhagen. The next night, Midsummer's Eve, everyone wanted to stay up late and burn bonfires the way we did every year. Of course, the Germans wouldn't allow it because of the blackout. So instead we planned a little surprise — for both the Germans and the Danes. My part in this was in Tivoli. I guess it was a little after eight-thirty when I arrived there and began strolling around looking for the perfect spot.

I had already walked through the fun fair,

past the rides, the huge roller coaster . . . the beautiful carousel with its giant animals: a giraffe, an elephant, a camel, horses, an ostrich. The giraffe was always my favourite; you had to climb a little ladder to get to your seat, which was very high up. Past the vendors selling candy and lollipops and ice cream . . . past the restaurants . . . past the gambling casino.

I stopped in front of the concert hall, an elegant, ornate building with a glass turret decorating the central entrance. Directly in front of the building was a lovely plot of flowerbeds, in the centre of which was a water fountain. That was my spot. I was dressed as a worker and I carried a tool bag in one hand and some flowering plants in the other. I marched into the centre of the flowerbed, made room for my geraniums, planted them, then looked around to check my position. Everything looked fine; no one was taking any notice of me.

Janicke was there, too. She had been keeping an eye open for Germans, and now she was making sure she was in the right place to get some good pictures. We were looking forward to *making* news for once, not just covering it — and this would definitely make news. Even in the official papers.

I knew there was a second team also in Tivoli, and a third one at the town hall. I had to coordinate with both of them, and I only had till nine p.m. to get set up. I took out my equipment and began to work quickly. I looked at my watch; it was five minutes to nine. At that moment two SS men strolled by. I stuck my head practically into the dirt, but they barely glanced at me. I hated to see them there, in Tivoli. Somehow they ruined it by their presence.

I had three minutes to go. I set my materials firmly into the ground, then made sure everything was all ready to be ignited. I signalled to Janicke and she walked away into the crowd. She couldn't be caught near the action. I checked my watch again. One minute. I began to light the fuses. There were twenty fuses in all, each of them a different length so they would detonate at thirty-second intervals. All done. I snapped my tool kit shut, got up and headed for the largest group of people, those milling around the line for the roller coaster. Then I heard it. The first hiss, then a whooshing sound. The crowd turned around, murmured, fearful of bombs. Someone screamed, parents grabbed their children, and then suddenly *BOOM!* The sky overhead exploded in a pure white shower of stardust. The crowd gasped with pleasure, and children squealed with delight. Then another one, *BOOM*, and again a rocket exploded, showering reds and blues and yellows. And the fireworks from the other squares exploded, too, until the whole sky was ablaze with colour, and for a while the only sounds were the hiss and boom of the rockets and the exultant cries of the crowd. Then people began cheering, and applauding each new burst, and one woman beside me started to cry. I slipped quietly through the throng and out into the street. Janicke was right where she'd said she'd be, snapping pictures.

Just then a whole group of the Schalburg Corps — our own Danish Nazis — came around the corner and headed toward us. I touched Janicke's arm. She put her camera in her bag and we sauntered away from there. I could hear the Schalburg Corps screaming and swearing, threatening to arrest everyone, racing into Tivoli to find the rockets. It would be too late by the time they did. They hated not being in control.

We got on a streetcar. The driver was having a hard time driving, he was so busy watching the fireworks. Finally he stopped the car so he could see, too. Everyone leaned out the windows, sighing and clapping. Janicke and I looked at each other and grinned.

"I think I got some beauties," she whispered, patting her bag with the camera inside it.

"Definitely front-page material," I agreed, a smile glued to my face. I felt like a tiny kid again, as if I could jump up and scream and clap and then thumb my nose at all those Germans and just run away, laughing. Laughing at them.

I had seen a little boy do that a few days earlier. He was only around ten and he made faces at the Germans and the Germans shot at him and he ran back and made more faces as they shot at him again. He did it four times in all, each time disappearing around a corner, until finally he was gone and they were standing in the street helpless, with these stupid expressions on their faces . . .

Suddenly there was music blaring. "It's a Long Way to Tipperary" piped through the town hall's public address system. Everyone in the streetcar roared with laughter, as did those on the street. Soon we were all singing along at the top of our lungs. A young boy jumped onto the streetcar and checked for Germans; seeing it was all clear, he passed out leaflets which

60

said that the fireworks were a greeting to the people of Copenhagen from fighting Denmark. The crowd on the streetcar applauded him as he waved to them and leaped off the streetcar.

Janicke leaned over, threw her arms around me, and gave me a big kiss on the cheek. At that moment I was sure I'd died and gone to heaven. Two teenage girls sitting behind us squealed with delight at the display. I felt that all Copenhagen was together, that for one magic moment we were all free.

6

"Kris, wake up!" I sat up quickly. I slept lightly — almost with one eye open. I had a little cot bed in the basement and I'd learned to sleep even if the press was in full swing. Sven was calling me from his desk, just hanging up the phone. He'd been travelling with this press from house to house, as had I, only he was a real journalist, absolutely tops — always cheerful, enthusiastic, laughing, and with his big round blue eyes managing to look as if he'd just woken up, even if he'd been awake two nights in a row.

He had a look of mixed emotions on his face; I could tell it was a good story but bad news. That was the strange thing about being a reporter. Some of our best stories contained some of the worst news.

"What?" I asked, trying desperately to look

and feel as alert as he was, but not being quite so successful now that I knew I'd been woken up for a story and not because the Gestapo had the house surrounded.

"It's Tivoli," he replied. "It's been Schalburgtaged." That's a new word in the Danish vocabulary. It means that the Schalburg Corps have ruined something and then tried to pretend it was the resistance who had done it — except most Danes know who's really to blame.

"There've been some big explosions. I want you to check it out."

I never knew if it was day or night there in the basement. The tiny windows were carefully blocked over with paper, then heavy cloth. As if anticipating my question, Sven continued, "It's four a.m. The explosions happened about two. Take your bike. Janicke will go with you. If you can be back before eight we can have this out today. The Germans are more stupid than I gave them credit for." He smiled.

I tried to smile back. I knew what he meant: The Danes loved Tivoli. The Germans might as well have blown up every single brewery and deprived us of our beer. You can only push a Dane so far. If this helped to wake up some people and get them moving, well, I tried to tell myself, it was worth it — but I loved Tivoli, too, and I could feel the anger welling up in me.

This is what the Germans call counter sabotage. We blow up something of theirs; they blow up something of ours. For instance, they shot eight saboteurs the day they blew up Tivoli. They'd already captured them and sentenced them to death, but then they'd waited, holding them as hostages. They executed them in retaliation for the gun factory sabotage.

I threw on my black turtleneck and black pants and black jacket — all new clothes provided by my resistance friends. I had just turned seventeen in December. I was only around five foot ten then and I figured I wouldn't grow any more, but all of a sudden I started to grow and by June I was over six feet and very skinny. It made me feel even more awkward around Janicke.

"Kris, are you ready?" she called down the stairs.

"Yes, right!"

I hurried upstairs. She was dressed in dark clothes, too, but in a black skirt, black stockings, and a dark blue blouse. It might be light before we got back and we didn't want to look like resistance fighters in the daylight.

We took as many back streets as possible, staying off Amagerbrogade until we had to cross the canal and then the big bridge connecting Amager with the rest of Copenhagen. We rode past the parliament buildings alongside the canal, past the national museum, and across Vestre Boulevard. We could hear and see the commotion up ahead.

We slipped into Tivoli by the side entrance at the corner. I had this terribly irrelevant thought that I wished we were going there together, Janicke and I, on a date.

Well, by that time I had a major crush on her. It was so strange — I mean, I would've done anything for five minutes alone with her, walking hand in hand in the moonlight in Tivoli. She never treated me like a kid. She joked with me and talked to me as if I were her age. After all, I thought, two years is no big deal. And she was so gorgeous — long, thick, chestnut hair, deep brown eyes, white teeth with a little space in between the two front ones and a smile that seemed to take up her whole face. And what a figure! I was in a constant torture of longing and guilt. Guilt because I sort of felt that Lisa and I were meant for each other — but Lisa was far away, and after that night in October of last year I knew all too well that any moment could be my last. I mean, I was seventeen and all I'd ever done was kiss one girl, Lisa, once. I was just a kid when the war started, and since then I hadn't exactly had time for romance. But I would make some time, if only Janicke would give me a chance. I was afraid to do or say anything, though; we had to work together and if she didn't feel the same way it could make things terribly uncomfortable. She was very artistic. She painted and sketched, and she was funny, too — she often did cartoons for our paper. In free moments she would draw caricatures of all of us. It was too bad we always had to rip them up in case we were raided by the Germans.

It was unsettling sharing a house with this beautiful girl. We all had our own rooms but we'd often meet in the hallway, in our pyjamas, on our way to the bathroom, and I know I always turned bright red. It never bothered Janicke. At least, she never looked self-conscious. We had our own kind of domestic routine — well, perhaps routine is the wrong word since we never ate our meals at the same time day to day, and sometimes we were too busy to eat. But Janicke cooked, I cleaned up, and we all kept the house in order. She made wonderful fish dishes when we could get fish; it was a real treat. We'd have great long talks, sitting at the table in the kitchen, drinking chicory instead of coffee since we couldn't get coffee, talking about the war and what we'd do when it was over. It was sometimes difficult to talk because we couldn't tell each other much about our own families or friends. Anything like that could prove dangerous if one of us was caught. Finally I would say goodnight to her, then go to bed and dream about her. And those dreams . . .

At any rate, as soon as we entered Tivoli we had to run up behind some ticket booths to hide from a group of firefighters we saw walking toward us. There were three of them, and as they walked past, I hissed, "Say, can you tell your fellow Danes what's happened?"

They stopped and two of them walked over to us; the other looked nervously around and stayed behind. Both Janicke and I had our hands on our guns which were in deep pockets in our jackets.

"Who are you?" asked the older man, suspiciously.

"Reporters," I whispered.

"Right, then," he said. "You tell your readers it's a big mess. The concert hall is completely destroyed; the blast was so bad it shattered all the glass. The gambling house is wrecked, and so are Danish House, Tivani Italy, the blue

67

cars, the bumper cars. Anything close to the explosion was destroyed."

I could hear from his tone of voice that he was furious.

"Look here," he continued, "there're Germans everywhere, but if you want to come to the truck I'll see what I can do about getting you in. Want pictures, do you?"

"We sure do," said Janicke, patting the bag with the camera in it.

"Come on then."

Well, in no time we were fixed up with fire-fighter's coats and hats. It was starting to get light now — just light enough for Janicke to use her camera. The firefighters took us back into Tivoli. We walked past all sorts of German soldiers but there were places that were clear of them, so Janicke took out her camera and got her shots. She got one of the bumper cars and one of what was left of the concert hall — just rubble, really. I thought of all the wonderful hours I had spent there and I felt sick, really sick.

We went back to the truck, changed, thanked the firefighters and returned to where we'd left our bikes. It was around five-thirty by then, and light. There were other people out on their bikes and the streetcars were beginning to move. We rode across Langebro Bridge back into Amager and we were just about to turn off onto one of the side streets when German cars roared up behind us and began to set up barricades. I could see they were doing the same thing a few blocks ahead of us. There was no use trying to bike down a side street; I could hear the cars and see them, too. What they would do was to cordon off a small area, make sure no one could escape, and then check everyone's papers. They almost always caught people in these roundups. I suppose at this hour they were hoping to catch people like us, going home after a good night's work.

I had my fake identity papers and so did Janicke. But she also had the bag with her camera in it, and her gun. And I had my gun.

It was early, so there weren't a lot of people to process. We moved apart so that they wouldn't notice the two of us dressed in dark colours and travelling together. I rode my bike to the barricade at the end of the street, as did Janicke behind me. I stopped, got off, gave them my papers. My gun felt like a huge weight; if they searched me it was all over. I wondered if it was bulging out of my jacket pocket. They looked my papers over and nodded. I could go. No wonder; Janicke had done the papers, and she had become an expert at it. I rode my bike through, then pretended to take a moment to put away my papers. I was prepared to shoot it out with them if they stopped Janicke. I knew they'd torture her and then kill her if they caught her. Our only chance was to fight.

I saw her leap lightly off her bicycle and smile at them. Then she did something that made me gasp.

"Here," I heard her say to a young soldier, "could you hold this?" And she handed him her bag. She found her identity papers in her skirt pocket and with another smile handed them to the other soldier. He checked them, nodded. She got on her bike and rode through the barricade, waving and wishing them, "Good morning." The young soldier was still holding her bag, grinning at her with a smitten look.

"Hey," shouted the other soldier when she had almost reached me, "you forgot your bag."

She turned quickly, rode back, stuck out her hand, and the young soldier gave it to her. As she was turning to go again, he seemed to wake up.

"Oh," he said, "I didn't check it. What's in it?"

"Nothing," she joked, winking at him. "Just a camera with all sorts of illegal pictures. And a gun, of course."

"Of course," laughed the soldier, as he turned back to check the others who were waiting.

I rode a bit ahead, then turned off into a safer street. We were home twenty minutes after that.

Sven roared with laughter when he heard the story, and I fell even more in love with Janicke than before.

7

It's strange, but the fonder I became of Janicke, the more I thought about Lisa and Stefan — and the more I thought about them and their family, the more I thought about my own family. I had managed to put thoughts of my mother and father out of my head for a while — it was too frustrating and painful to think about — but that June, when it really began to look as if the war might end and I might get to see them again, I started to think about them all the time. I wondered if they had been questioned, if they were under surveillance. I tried to think of a way to find out. Finally I decided that one day I'd simply ride my bicycle past their street, to see if they were being watched. If it looked clear, I'd sneak in at night and visit them. If I could just let them know I was alive, I knew it would help both them and me.

On the Monday after our Tivoli adventure, I mulled over when I should go. It was late afternoon and I was folding the newspapers and putting them neatly in rows in large boxes. All day, and the day before, too, we had worked on a special edition of the paper. It included our story about Tivoli and some more big news which had broken on Sunday.

Dr. Best, who is the German commander here in Denmark, had declared a curfew from eight p.m. to five a.m. It was to begin on Monday. In response, the workers at our biggest shipyard, Burmeister and Wain, had written Dr. Best a very polite letter. In it they had told him that they'd be forced to quit work at noon, starting Monday, and every day thereafter. A lot of workers had small vegetable plots in communal gardens and the letter stated that they needed enough time to cultivate them. If they had to be indoors by eight p.m. they would just have to begin earlier. It was not a strike, they explained; they would simply be forced to work fewer hours. This teasing kind of letter, this resistance that pretended not to be resistance, must have driven the Germans absolutely crazy. After all, the ships these workers were building were very important to the Germans. The late-breaking news was that the workers had indeed walked out at noon, as promised. We managed to add an extra page for that story.

We were working to a strict deadline. The papers would be picked up at six p.m.; then they'd be put on trains or boats for Sweden, or distributed to kids here in Copenhagen who would give them out door to door. We also had a mailing list of about a hundred subscribers.

The paper looked great. The front page had a dramatic picture of the concert hall in ruins with jagged, cracked glass jutting everywhere — almost like a modern painting — and one of the bumper cars all twisted and bent. Then it had my story on the inner page, and on the third page the story about the workers at the shipyard.

"It's time to think about moving," Sven declared, out of the blue. Janicke and I were just sealing the boxes, which were marked and disguised as school supplies.

"Why?" she asked sharply.

"Our neighbour across the street," he replied, with his ever-present laugh. "He likes me too much. He's gotten *so* friendly, so interested; he rattles on about the rotten Germans, how wonderful the resistance is, how he'd *love* to help. What if I were a German informer? If he really wanted to help he wouldn't be so open. He'd be more cautious, a little remark here and there, see how I respond, and if I responded well, he'd say a little more. No, this guy acts as if he'd have nothing to lose if he were caught. It's only a feeling, but I don't like it."

Just then we heard a knock at the door. It was our new code, four quick, two slow. Janicke and I covered the door, guns ready, as Sven opened it. It was Paul, our courier. He was parked out front. We had debated whether to move the boxes in broad daylight or late at night, but now, with the curfew, late at night would seem even more suspicious. Instead we acted as if there were nothing to hide. The car was packed in a minute, each of us carrying out one box, and it drove off. We had told the neighbours that we operated a small school-supply business from the house so we were able to do this, and to come and go as needed. People were out on the streets, coming home from work, and with all the hustle and bustle nobody seemed to take any notice of us. But then I glanced at the house across the street and saw the curtain flutter. I felt sure someone had been watching.

We got back in and Sven said, "I'm going to find us another safe house. In the meantime you start packing."

I groaned. *Packing*. I knew what that meant. It meant taking the damned press apart. Would I be able to sneak out later, I wondered, and check on my family? What if our new safe house was in the country? If I didn't go tonight I might not get another chance in the near future. I set to work, directing Janicke, who knew less about the way the press fitted together, and within an hour and a half we had it ready to be moved. Sven still had no place for us to go. He was on the phone — through our connections at the phone exchange we had a secure number — and he was checking around.

"I'll be back in an hour," I told Janicke quietly. I tucked my gun into the waistband of my trousers and put on my jacket to cover the bulge. I couldn't ask Sven's permission in case he refused. I didn't give Janicke a chance to object either. I slipped out quickly without Sven's noticing, and I took my bike and headed downtown. The city was in a mad rush, especially in the downtown streets, with everyone trying to get home before the eight o'clock curfew. I travelled down Gothersgade to Kronprinsessegade and then onto Sølvgade and finally onto Øster Sogade. At this point I slowed down and looked for anything suspicious. Our apartment was just down the street. There were no black cars stationed nearby, no patrols loitering . . . The Needle was probably right. I was small potatoes; they wouldn't waste manpower on me. Probably they'd forgotten all about me and hadn't ever bothered with my family.

Suddenly it occurred to me that the safest thing to do, if I was determined to see them, was to see them right then. After all, at this hour the streets were packed with people, there would be kids running in and out of the apartment block, whereas after curfew I would stick out dangerously. I decided to do it. I parked my bike at the apartment block just beside ours. The water in the lake across the street shone in the late afternoon sun. People were out rowing. For a moment it felt as though nothing had changed and I was just a kid hurrying home for a late dinner.

I walked quickly down the street and in a moment I was at our building. I slipped in the front door, into the foyer. Our apartment was the first one on the right. I was lucky. There was no one in the foyer. I knocked lightly on the door. No one answered. I was in a fit of nerves; I was sweating and my heart was pounding. I don't know whether I was scared of being caught, or excited about seeing them, or nervous that they wouldn't be home, or all of these put together.

The front door of the apartment building crashed open and four boys, all around seven or eight, stormed into the foyer and made for the stairs, talking, laughing and still playing with their soccer ball. I knocked again, louder, and the door opened a crack. I heard my mother gasp. She opened the door, pulled me in, slammed the door behind me. She tried to call for my father but no words would come out. For a moment she didn't even hug me. She just stood there staring at me. She looked older. Her hair had more grey in it and her cheeks had lost some of their rosy colour. Tears welled up in her eyes and started to roll down her cheeks. I suddenly felt as if *I* were the parent, as if I needed to protect and comfort *her*. And that made me feel very sad.

"Mom," I said, "are you all right?"

Then she gave me a hug, but not a big one — a tentative hug, as if she couldn't believe I was really there.

"Dad!" I called.

My father appeared in the hallway. He was

tall and lanky and it seemed to me he'd got thinner all over, even his hair.

"Jesper!" he exclaimed, and he came over and gave me a huge hug and a big kiss. "Jesper!"

Oh boy, it was good to hear my real name again.

"It's all right, Mom, I'm all right," I tried to reassure her. She was crying and trembling. My father and I led her into the living room and we all sat down on the couch. She took my hand. I gave her a kiss.

My father shook his head. "We thought they'd caught you."

"They did catch me," I said, "the night I disappeared."

My mother's grasp tightened on my hand. "But I was rescued, and I've been underground ever since. I just wanted to let you know that I'm alive. I was afraid to earlier. They could have been watching you — or they may have a neighbour spying on you. I thought I might have been recognized the night I was captured."

"We were never questioned," my father said.

I wanted to tell them about Frederik but I wasn't sure I should. After all, if he was with the resistance and under deep cover, the fewer people who knew, the better. On the other hand, if he really was a Nazi he was the reason I'd been forced underground, and I wanted to tell my parents that. But in the end I decided that the less they knew, the safer they'd be.

My mother finally spoke, her voice choked, a whisper.

"Look how you've grown. Look at you. You're all grown up. How do you live? How do you eat?"

"I live with some great people," I said. "Don't worry. We have lots to eat, probably more than you. We just print our own ration cards."

"But you're too thin," she objected.

I glanced at my father. "I don't think I'm going to grow out of that."

Finally she permitted herself a small smile.

My father was positively beaming.

"I can't stay," I said abruptly, wanting nothing more at that moment than to pretend I'd never been captured and forced to live underground. I wanted to go to sleep in my own bed, and to go to school in the morning and to start studying English literature again. I wanted my mother to take care of me and baby me; regret poured over me as I understood that would never happen again. And I felt doubly confused when I realized that Frederik probably hadn't recognized me, that perhaps I'd gone underground for nothing. For a split second then I tried to convince myself it wasn't too late to come home. But Janicke and Sven were waiting for me and I couldn't just turn my back on them. I didn't really want to. In a way, they were my family now, too.

My mother was holding my hand so tightly that I couldn't get it away.

"Oh, Mom, I could use that hand," I joked, "if it wasn't broken."

"What? Oh!" she exclaimed, loosening her grip.

Gently I pulled my hand away and got up. "I have to get back before curfew." I looked at my watch. It was seven-thirty.

"Yes, yes, of course you do," said my father, and I saw tears in his eyes. Not too clearly, though, because my eyes were all teary, too — I was trying very hard not to cry.

"The war news is good," said my father, encouraging me. "We'll see you soon."

"We could hide you here," said my mother, her face hopeful.

I shook my head. "You know that would never work. Some nosy neighbour could give us all away. And anyway, I have work to do."

I gave her a big hug, my father, too. Then I ran. I felt that if I stayed another minute I wouldn't have the courage to leave again. I burst out of the apartment, forgetting to check that it was clear first.

A young man and woman were just coming into the foyer, neighbours from one floor up. They looked at me in shock. "Jesper!"

I said hello, then hurried out and away. I grabbed my bike and rode as quickly as I could. I got back just before eight. It was odd ,but the streets were still full of people, despite the fact that the curfew was about to begin.

I checked in with Sven.

"Where have you been?" he asked.

"To see my parents," I replied.

For a moment I thought he was going to murder me, he looked so angry. And Sven almost never looked angry. Then his face broke into his usual smile.

"How are they?"

"Fine," I said. "They've had no trouble. It may be safe for me to surface."

"Do you want to?"

"I never thought I had a choice," I answered slowly. "Now that I might be able to, I really don't want to."

I don't think I realized at the time how much the thought of leaving Janicke affected my decision. In fact, it was never much of a choice in my mind. I wanted to stay. I felt that I was helping get rid of the Germans. And, even if I didn't admit it to myself, I also wanted to stay because of Janicke. I wanted to be near her every minute, every second, and even the pull of my own mother and father wasn't strong enough to change that. Still, it was disturbing to think that perhaps I'd gone underground for nothing.

"Any trouble on the way?" he asked.

"No. Except . . ."

"What?"

"Well, I got here just at eight and the streets were still packed with people."

We went and looked out the front window. It was five past eight and half the neighbourhood was still outside.

"What about the curfew?" I asked.

"Don't know," he replied. "I've arranged for a car to pick us up here at one a.m. In the meantime, why don't you go out and see what's happening?"

8

It was a gorgeous night. The air was warm; it smelled sweet, of flowers. But because of the curfew, parents should have been hustling their children inside. Everyone should have been in a hurry to get off the streets. Instead, although I saw the little ones being taken in for bed; the teenagers were out hanging around, talking; the adults were still working on their flowers, pruning their shrubbery, talking to neighbours, taking strolls. The houses in the area were quite big and well kept. They were made out of red, orange, or yellow brick, with red clay roofs, and had lots of lawn, large gracious trees, flowers. Sven's parents had moved to Aarhus just before our last move, and they'd given him the house. He could never have afforded it on the wages of a lowly reporter. They also sent him money, and he'd been more or less supporting us all that time.

I smiled and said hello to our next-door neighbours, a young couple with a little baby who cried all night, every night. They were pruning some bushes in the front yard.

"Lovely night," said the woman.

"How's the baby?" I asked.

"It's colic, you know," she said. "She's asleep now but she'll be up in an hour, then off and on all night." She grinned. "But I suppose you know that."

I laughed. "I can sleep through anything." I paused. "There's a curfew tonight, you know," I said casually. After all, maybe they just hadn't heard about it.

They both looked at each other, then at me. I knew what they were thinking. Who was I? Was I a German informer? Was I dangerous to them, to their baby?

"Oh? Is there?" said the young man. "Dear me. Well, it's not until eight and look at my watch" — he showed me — "it's only seven."

"Oh, you're right," I answered. "Mine must be wrong." I pretended to set mine back and I smiled. "That must be the correct time. Well, enjoy the evening."

It was now well after eight and no one was

moving indoors. I walked over to a group of kids who looked about fourteen years old — three girls and a boy. They were sitting on the grass, poring over a magazine filled with pictures of Nelson Eddy and Jeanette Macdonald. Nelson Eddy was looking as romantic as usual in his Royal Canadian Mounted Police uniform. The girls were swooning and even the boy looked awfully envious.

"Hi!" I said.

"Oh," they said, "hi!"

"It's late," I commented.

"Is it?" they said, and then went back to their discussion. "Are they in love in real life?" said one of the girls.

A police car drove slowly down the street and stopped quite near us. Two old men were standing on the sidewalk, smoking pipes and talking. The police got out of their car and went up to them. They were Danish police; most of them hated helping the Germans, and they often used their position to help fellow Danes.

"Time to go in!" one of them announced. "Or I'll have to arrest you! Orders!" He was young, maybe in his early twenties, and he didn't look too happy about what he had to do.

"Oh! Officer!" said one of the men. "I didn't know I was out."

"What?" said the policeman.

"Why, what am I doing out?" said the old man. He looked around, seeming totally confused. "Why, I must have been walking in my sleep."

I had a hard time keeping a straight face. I almost choked, trying not to laugh.

The policeman opened his mouth to reply but couldn't think of anything to say. His companion, a more seasoned veteran, took a different approach.

"Get into your houses," he demanded. "At once! Or I'll arrest you for breaking curfew."

"Why, of course, sir, at once!" the old man replied. And slowly, ever so slowly, he started to shuffle back to his house. At this rate, I thought, it'll take him until morning to get to his front door.

The policeman looked around in frustration at everyone out in the street.

"Now everyone go inside!" he shouted. "Curfew began at eight."

No one moved. They all continued to do exactly what they'd been doing. I couldn't believe my eyes.

Finally the older one rushed down the street toward the young couple. The woman moved toward the house, thinking of her baby, no doubt. The man continued to clip his hedge.

"You! Into your house!" the policeman yelled. The young man looked at him calmly.

Slowly, the people on the street gathered around the policeman and the young man.

"Look," the young man said, "don't get mixed up in this. Let the Germans do their own dirty work."

The crowd closed in and muttered agreement.

The older policeman looked at the younger one. "You know," he said, "I think this young fella may just be right." He nudged his partner, and they turned and walked back to their car.

Suddenly I heard shooting. It seemed to be coming from the street parallel to ours, Tønnesvej. I slipped through the houses and onto Tønnesvej in time to see two German soldiers riding their motorbikes and firing at people at random. It was the strangest thing I'd ever seen: although some people ran behind trees, fences, even houses, for cover, no one went back inside. Then, *thunk* — one of the soldiers was hit by a chamber pot, a full chamber pot someone had thrown from a window. He was covered in the contents of the pot, he was soaking wet. He dropped his machine gun, and sputtered and screamed. Then he grabbed his machine gun, turned on the house he thought the offending "weapon" had been thrown from, and fired. He shot out all the windows. Still no one ran back inside.

What was happening? Was all of Copenhagen in revolt?

I ran back to Jansvej, the street I lived on. People were dragging things to the top of the street. The teenagers were helping. I ran up to them. They had handcarts, old bicycles, one even had a small chest of drawers. They piled it all across the street as a barricade. Soon they were joined by others and I could see the same thing happening at the other end of the street. It was simply incredible. No one was even considering going in. They were just trying to make sure they kept the Germans out. And everyone was talking and laughing. There was a spark here I hadn't felt in years — as if it were a big festival or holiday.

Well, I started to wander from street to street then, talking to people, finding out what was happening. As the sky darkened, people lit the barricades at the ends of their streets and huge bonfires blazed. Firefighters put them out only to see them relit. I knew I had until around twelve-thirty before I had to return home, so I stayed out, in the shadows, talking to people and scripting a great story for the next day's paper.

Finally, around midnight, I decided it was time to go back to Sven's house. Jansvej seemed very quiet, more so than the other streets where people were still out. As I approached the house a chill ran down my spine. I didn't know why, but suddenly I was alert and nervous. Instead of going right up to the door I approached the house cautiously, going around to the back. I checked all the windows, and that's when I saw something I didn't like. No, I didn't like it at all. There was a small slit of light in the basement window. We were always terribly careful not to let even a crack of light out, because anyone who looked in would see the printing press. I felt in my gut that something was wrong. But what? And what should I do? I took my gun out.

What was that? I could hear a rustling; it was soft and distinct. Someone was coming. I crouched down by a bush, trying to get behind it, but the person was too close. All of a sudden there was a gun in my face.

"Shoot and you're dead," the words hissed at me.

It was Janicke.

"Janicke," I whispered, "please don't shoot me, please!"

"You idiot! I've been looking everywhere for you."

"I just got back," I replied. "What's going on?"

"It's thanks to you, actually," she whispered, "that I wasn't caught. I went out looking for you. I thought we could work on this story together. When I came back there were Germans everywhere. They've got Sven in there. They're just waiting for more of us to show up. I want to get him out."

A place in the pit of my stomach knotted up as I pictured that ride to Ryvangen again; I knew I was sweating, and I had a terrible urge to leave Sven and to run and get away. I took a deep breath and thought of the roller coaster.

"Got any ideas?" I said.

"There are two SS men in there with him now, but I'm sure there are cars hidden around here somewhere to catch us if we try to escape. We'll have to cut through the houses and get ourselves onto a street where there are lots of people out, and bonfires, and get lost in the crowds. The Germans will be slowed down by the bonfires. I've got the address of our new safe house. It's in Amager but close to downtown. It's an apartment."

"But what about Sven?" I asked.

"If one of us knocks, they'll let him open the door to lure us in. The person who knocks has to grab Sven, pull him out, and shut the door. That'll slow them down for a few seconds. Then we run. There's a bonfire two streets over. We can cut right through there." She pointed.

"All right," I answered, "I'll knock. You cover me."

We crept softly around the back, and Janicke stood on one side of the door. I knocked — four quick, two slow — my heart pounding so hard I couldn't tell if I'd knocked the correct number. There was a pause. Then the door opened. Fortunately it was the kind of door that opens out. I took Sven's hand and pulled him past the door, out of their line of fire, and slammed it shut. I could hear them swear, and then they started to fire through the door.

"Run!" Janicke ordered.

We sprinted across the back lawn and into the next street as headlights came on behind us, and more guns opened up. We dashed across that street and past the next set of houses, and finally into a street awash in the eerie light of a bonfire. People were milling about, singing; some were dancing. It flashed through my mind that our being there wasn't such a good idea. We were putting all these people in danger. We raced through the crowds to the end of the street, where a Danish police car was parked. Two policemen were standing around, looking helpless. They saw our guns and reached for theirs, but slowly, almost as if they weren't really trying.

"Throw them down," Sven yelled.

They did.

"Keys!" he demanded, pointing his gun at one of them. The policeman handed him the keys, and as he did so said, "And good luck to you."

"Thanks," replied Sven as we threw ourselves into the car. The car had real gasoline in it, and we took off, with Sven driving, and headed away from there as fast as we could.

We passed some Germans and other police but nobody raised the alarm, as they just assumed we were Danish police. It was too dark to see that we weren't in uniform.

"What are we going to do without our press!" Sven exclaimed, really angry.

"We'll find something," I assured him, smiling to myself. He was more worried about that hunk of machinery than he was thankful that we were all alive.

"First thing I'd like to do," Janicke said

grimly, "is take care of our good neighbour across the street."

"The resistance won't let us do it," Sven commented. "But," he added cheerfully, "they'll make sure someone else does."

I wondered what our neighbour would get in payment for his tip to the Gestapo. A dozen eggs? Money? Or was it just the prestige, just the thanks from his masters for a job well done?

9

Someone is knocking on the cell wall. I go to listen. "Don't give up" is the message. "It's almost over."

I knock back, "I won't give up."

It's true, I think. The war is almost over. But it will be too late for me. I wonder what time it is. I think the last meal they gave me was a noon meal. It must be sometime in the late afternoon.

I want to organize this next section in my head before I sleep. Where is this part of the story heading? I guess I'm heading for the part where I realized — no, where I *felt*, deep inside me — that this was no longer a game. It all became too real. And yet, everything was still black and white. We were the good guys, they were the bad guys. It wasn't until later that I found things getting complicated — later being now. Now I'm confused, but then everything was simple. Good against evil. Simple.

Janicke, Sven, and I ended up in the new safe house, an apartment this time. We were still on the island of Amager. Our hostess was a middle-aged housewife, Hanne, whose children were in the country with relatives and whose husband was one of the military arrested in August 1943. He was in a concentration camp — may still be. We all felt miserable about leaving the press behind. And what an unbelievable story there was to put out! But Hanne had a best friend who worked in the phone exchange, so at least we had a secure line almost immediately. Sven got on the phone and started gathering information, as if we could still somehow get a paper out. I began composing a story in my head about what I'd seen the night before.

Then the phone rang. Sven answered. He looked at me and with raised eyebrows handed me the phone.

I couldn't imagine who would know I was there — after all, we'd just arrived . . .

"Yes?" I said into the mouthpiece.

"Kris?" said a voice.

"Yes."

"You're to meet us tonight, at Lena ten-twenty. We have some precious cargo arriving and need some help making sure it isn't intercepted."

I paused, unsure. Could it really be someone from my old sabotage group? How did they know where to find me?

"Birds fly free, Kris," said the voice.

That was our code. No one else knew it. Unless one of them had been captured and had talked.

"What time?" I asked.

"One a.m.," said the voice. "See you." And he rang off.

First rule: if you are going somewhere with a different group, don't tell the group you're with, as it only endangers them.

"I have to be somewhere tonight," I replied to Janicke and Sven, whose faces were full of questions. I turned to Sven.

"How could anyone know I'm here?"

"It's not that strange," he replied. "I made a lot of calls before someone found us this place — and everything is so centralized now, they probably know where everyone is. Just a matter of the right person asking the right question. But," he added, "be careful, just in case."

I went to look for the telephone book. Our code worked by letters and numbers connected to the phone book. "Lena ten-twenty" turned out to be Hellerup leisure-craft harbour: a small harbour right in the centre of Copenhagen where people moored their sail-boats. For some reason the Germans had no patrols there, I suppose because all the waters were so heavily patrolled that they felt it was unnecessary. But I knew that the resistance used it a lot for smuggling people in and out of Copenhagen. By bike the trip would take me around three-quarters of an hour. I had to decide which was more dangerous — riding there after curfew, or riding there now and hanging around until one a.m. There were houses and apartments there, but no real places to hide. I decided to wait until just after midnight, and to go then. Hanne offered me her bicycle.

I spent the rest of the day in an agony of sus-pense. I wrote out the story from the night before in longhand, since Hanne didn't have a typewriter. That, at least, kept me busy. When I'd finished that I cleaned my gun. Three times.

Janicke told me not to go. She didn't like it. But I had to.

At eight o'clock we all went to the window. We were on the third floor; the window overlooked the street, and we were just in the middle of the block, so we had an excellent view. I was very curious as to what would happen with the curfew. Sven had found out, through his calls, that more and more businesses had closed that day. The strike that wasn't a strike was spreading right through Copenhagen. And sure enough, the street was still full of people. They wandered around, chatted, visited. Some carried old mattresses, handcarts, baskets, anything they could spare, and they piled it up at one end of the street. Others did the same at the opposite end of the street. Then suddenly a black car arrived at one end of the street. The people ducked behind their barricades as the car slowed down and machine-gun fire sprayed everywhere. But as soon as the car disappeared, the people rushed to the barricade and set it alight. Soon a huge bonfire blocked the street. Everyone began to sing. Our window was open and the strains of the music wafted in along with the heavy, humid evening air.

Janicke and I badly wanted to go down there. She wanted pictures; I wanted a story. But

Sven told us that we had strict orders to remain out of sight.

Instead we all stayed at the windows. In fact, almost all the windows on the street were open — another act of defiance, as we had been ordered to have them shut and well covered for the blackout. I could see the flicker of bonfires on other streets, could hear a cacophony of sounds: shooting, singing, fire engines. The sky meanwhile was getting darker and darker, until suddenly the clouds opened up. Thunder crashed, lightning flashed, and a truly terrible storm blasted the city. That drove everyone inside, and although the prospect of riding through that downpour wasn't very appealing, I realized that I'd be much safer. In such a torrent of rain I would be difficult to see — especially all dressed in black. I decided to leave a little early, as I knew it would take me longer to struggle there through the storm.

What a night that was! Within a minute of leaving the apartment I was drenched to the bone. My bike slid around under me, and although I couldn't easily be seen, I could see very little myself. Halfway there I almost drove right into a German patrol before I noticed their car lights. I slid and slipped into a side street and waited in a doorway for a few minutes, then ventured out again. The city was silent, the storm having driven both demonstrators and Germans inside. I finally reached the harbour at about ten to one, a good hour and a half after I'd set out. It was black, and it was quiet. At the end of the pier one dim little light shone on the small lighthouse. I ran down to the pier. Seeing no one, I jumped into a small rowboat moored there, just so I wouldn't be so obvious. I waited. I was soaked, shivering, cold, miserable. Was it a trap? Was I about to be captured once again?

I heard a thin whistle then: one long note, two short.

That was our old signal. When Stefan, Per, Jens, Susanne and Lisa and I used to work together, that whistle always meant the coast is clear, let's get going. It had to be either Per or Jens whistling, since there was no one else from our group left in Copenhagen. I could see a boat slowly, silently moving in through the downpour to dock. From out of the darkness a figure appeared on the pier and moved toward the boat. I took a deep breath and then did the same. My gun at the ready, I ran toward the boat, reaching it at the same time as the other person. He came right up to me, slapped me on the back, and whispered, "Nice to see you again, Jesper." I could just make out that it was Jens. We'd always used our real names among ourselves, because we'd all been friends together; code names would have been pointless. We shook hands warmly, then turned our attention to the boat. It was a motorboat, and it was manoeuvring up the quay, squeezing in between two large fishing boats.

Someone threw a line. I caught it and tied it to a pole on the dock. I could see someone on board shake hands with the captain. Suddenly four more people were behind us on the pier: two men carrying large parcels in their arms, one woman, and another man carrying a child whose mouth was taped shut. It was a little boy and it looked to me as if he'd been given an injection, as he was limp and pale. The person on the boat jumped onto the dock, and the four people on the pier scrambled into the boat, handing their precious cargo to the crew on board. The rain lessened from a downpour to a steady drizzle.

Something in my stomach twisted as a blond young man leaped from the boat, landing between Jens and myself. I had no time to pay attention to anything, however, except getting that boat away safely and getting our new arrival out of danger as well.

"Is that all?" I asked Jens.

"Yes."

I untied the line and we pushed the boat out of its berth. Two crewmen rowed it out of the harbour. The dim glow of the lighthouse caught our new arrival's blond hair.

"Don't you have a cap?" I hissed. "You might as well be wearing a street lamp!"

He smothered a laugh, pulled a cap out of his pocket, and covered his hair. He seemed to have a blond moustache, too, and glasses, but that was all I could tell.

"Come on," Jens whispered. "I have a car. We'll all go together."

"What about my bike?" I asked.

"Go get it, we'll put it in the back."

I did so and we all piled into the car — Jens driving, me in the passenger seat, the new arrival between us.

"Where are we going?" I asked Jens.

"I'll take you back to Amager," he answered. "You're safe there for the moment. Then I'll be in touch. There must be something special planned."

Just then the moon came out from behind the clouds and our new arrival turned to me.

My stomach dropped as if I were diving from a three-storey building, and despite my best efforts I could feel tears in my eyes.

It was Stefan!

"Lisa sends her love," he said.

10

"Lisa," I repeated. "Is she all right?"

"She's fine," he grinned, and then I realized I hadn't even greeted him. Neither of us knew whether to hug each other, which seemed babyish, or to shake hands, which didn't seem right for two friends who were as close as brothers, so we didn't do either. We just sat there like idiots, grinning at each other.

Stefan slipped his hand into his jacket pocket and when he brought it out he dropped a small paper bag into my palm.

"Couldn't come for a visit without bringing your favourite."

I reached into the bag and felt about a dozen small hard candies. I popped two into my mouth. The taste of licorice exploded on my tongue.

"Thanks," I said with feeling, putting the bag carefully into my pants pocket.

"Rock candy for Jens," he said and drew another bag out of his jacket.

"Aah," Jens sighed with delight, sticking it in his jacket. "I'll save these for later, when I can really savour them."

"Now look," I chided, "why did you do it, you moron?" and I hit him on the shoulder. "You were safe, you were free, you were one less person for me to worry about . . ."

"I had to, Jesper," he said, suddenly dead serious. "Couldn't stay there safe and sound with all this" — he gestured round him — "going on."

"But how did you convince them?"

Stefan darted a sly look at Jens. "Between friends?"

Jens and I answered together, "Between friends."

"I lied about my age. Told them I was twenty."

Jens burst out laughing. "And they're so stupid they believed you?"

"Come on," I pressed, "it had to be more than that. The higher-ups aren't that blind."

"Agreed," Stefan nodded. "But they knew that I was dead serious about getting back here — and there's something special they need me for. They want us working together again, the three of us plus a couple more if we can manage it. I have a special job for us."

This brought me back to reality and I was abruptly aware that it was late — very late. We had no business being out on the streets and if we met a German patrol now we'd never even get to hear about Stefan's plan. Jens was driving through small residential streets, trying to keep off the main thoroughfares. The sky had cleared, and with the moon shining through the front window I could see Stefan better. His auburn hair was now very blond. He had a light blond moustache and very thin glasses which showed up his blue eyes. His skin had always been very light, and with his high cheekbones and full mouth he looked as if he'd stepped right out of a German propaganda poster.

"Is that moustache yours?" I asked, trying to keep my tone nonchalant and not sound terribly envious.

"What do you think?"

"No!" I grabbed it and pulled.

"Aaah!" He stifled a scream. Then he pummelled me on my arm. "Yes, you idiot, it's real!"

"Oh." I smiled. "Sorry."

"I'll bet you are."

I laughed. I was shaving by then, but I still couldn't grow a really good moustache like that. I'd check every morning to see if it was getting thicker but nothing much was happening.

Jens muttered, "Jesper, get your gun ready. Stefan, have you got one?"

"Yes," he replied. A black car was heading toward us, a machine gun sticking out of one of its windows. We were quiet, Stefan and I taking the safety off our guns, then holding them carefully under our jackets.

The car swerved in front of us, stopped, and two big — no, huge — Gestapo goons jumped out and, pointing their machine guns, raced over to us.

Jens spoke very quietly. "They look trigger-happy. No use trying to talk this one out. Roll down windows *now*, shoot on my say." I felt myself get that kind of icy calm that can come over you in a crisis. There was no time to think or feel, only to do.

Jens and I rolled down our windows. Stefan and I pulled out our guns, keeping them low and out of sight. The Germans arrived at our car and one of them shouted, *"Heraus!"*

"Yes, sir," Jens replied in German. As he said

it he leaned back to give Stefan a clear shot. I aimed for the heart and shot — four or five times at least — and I heard Stefan shoot, and I saw them both drop. Jens put his foot on the gas and we screeched away. I put the safety back on my gun and pushed it into my inside jacket pocket. We were all quiet for a long time.

Blowing up a factory and shooting a man who is close enough to touch are two very different things. I remember feeling a wave of disgust wash over me. And a wave of hate. I didn't hate myself — I knew it was him or me — but I hated the guy I'd shot; I hated the Germans for turning me into a killer. I knew that if it hadn't been for the Germans I would still be a school kid, nose stuck in my books, not even willing to crush a spider walking across my schoolroom desk. I felt cold inside, like ice. Calm and cold. I wondered how Jens and Stefan were taking it.

Grimly I said to Stefan, "Welcome home."

I could see his hands were shaking.

"Good to be here," he replied, attempting to smile but failing miserably. I knew he wouldn't try to speak again until he sounded more in control.

We were terribly tense, watching for more Gestapo cars, anxious to return to the apartment. We crossed the Knippels Bridge and were back in Amager. Jens turned off Amagerbrogade onto Aalandsgade, a smaller street running in the same direction.

"Do you have anyone we can use for this operation?" Stefan asked finally, his voice strained but steady.

"Depends what it is," I replied. "I'm working with two newspaper buffs now. They wouldn't be much good at sabotage but they're quick and smart."

"Well," Stefan said, and he seemed much older to me, all grown up, but I guess I must have seemed that way to him, too, "it's a rescue operation. It's the Needle. He's been captured."

"Not again!" I interjected.

"Again?"

"Oh, it's a long story. I'll tell you later."

"All right," he continued, "he's been captured, and he's in Rigshospitalet, and we have to get him out."

I knew then why Stefan was here. His father used to be a surgeon at Rigshospitalet before he had to flee to Sweden, and Stefan knew that place inside out. Also he had lots of friends there — nurses and orderlies — people who liked him and trusted him and would be willing to help if he asked, but might not be so willing to help a stranger. They knew they could trust Stefan.

"Right," he said, reading my look, "that's really why they ignored my age."

"I'm in," Jens said.

Jens was the oldest of us, twenty I'd say. He worked as an apprentice in a furniture factory; he was an incredible craftsman. He was very short and he had curly brown hair and a round face. He was terribly shy with girls and not too talkative around boys either. But he was brave as anything, calm, cool under pressure, and I'd rather have him on a mission with me than just about anyone.

As we got closer to my apartment block I directed Jens to slow down. He stopped a block away.

"You'd better drop us here," I said. "It's safer. How do I get in touch with you?"

"I'll call you tomorrow," he replied. "You set up a place to meet. Let me know by code, I'll be there. Your apartment might be the best place. I can get in. I'll get hold of a mailman's uniform or something like that."

"Right," I agreed. "Talk to you tomorrow."

"Good to have you back, Stefan," Jens said. "Sorry your first night worked out the way it did."

Stefan nodded, shook Jens' hand, and we got out of the car. We got the bike out. I rode on the sidewalk and Stefan jogged beside me. All was quiet. The bonfires were dead.

We reached the apartment block safely and silently ascended the three flights to the apartment. I unlocked the door and we moved into the dark foyer. Suddenly there was a gun in my stomach. A light flashed into my face, then into Stefan's.

"Just checking," laughed Sven as he turned off the flashlight. "Who's your friend?"

"Bjørn," answered Stefan, using a code name.

"And he is my friend," I added.

"Fine then," said Sven, "I'm off to sleep. See you in the morning."

"This way," I whispered to Stefan, and we stumbled our way through the living room into the kitchen. I felt my way over to the window, checked the curtains to see that no light would escape, and turned on a small lamp.

I stared at him. I really couldn't believe he was there. For a moment neither of us spoke, but I had an incredible urge to give him a big hug. Finally I grabbed him and did just that. He hugged me back, then we both laughed, and the tension was gone. I opened the icebox and we found some cold beer, a real treat.

"Hanne insists we help ourselves," I said. "I don't know where she gets so much of the stuff."

Stefan grinned. "I won't say no." We changed into some dry clothes. Then we sat down at the kitchen table to get caught up on the last nine months.

I didn't want to sleep anyway. If I slept, I'd dream about killing, about the man I'd killed that night. Stefan and I wouldn't talk about it. We both knew we had had no choice. But that didn't make the dreams go away.

11

It was wonderful to have Stefan back. I felt as if, I don't know, as if we could get through anything together. That night we talked until dawn. He told me that his father was working in a hospital in Stockholm, his mother had found a post at the university there, and Lisa was studying very hard — she wanted to study medicine. He said she felt frustrated at being kept out of her country and felt so helpless that she was pouring all her energies into her studies.

Lisa had never once mentioned to me that she wanted to be a doctor. I thought back to the last night that I'd seen her, how she'd shot a German soldier. Did she, I wondered, feel she had some lives to make up for? But she'd helped to save so many before she'd left. Just thinking about her made me feel guilty. How could I have let my feelings for Janicke get so strong?

I told Stefan about what I'd been doing and about my interest in journalism. He said he'd been training with the Danish Brigade, a fighting force of exiled Danes in Sweden. They were getting ready to join the Allied troops for the liberation of Denmark when the time came. It was fantastic to hear him speak — it wasn't "if" any more, it was "when." We talked about the spontaneous general strike, too. He had heard all about it in Sweden! The underground presses were getting the story out and the world press was gobbling it up. It went perfectly with the D-Day invasion as a propaganda piece against the Germans. It was front-page news all over the world.

At that point we got a little more personal. Stefan told me that Lisa worried about me constantly.

"I'm glad *she's* safe," I replied. Then I waited a bit and added, "Does she have any boyfriends?"

I don't know what I hoped he'd answer. If he said yes I wouldn't have to feel guilty about Janicke. But I knew I'd feel upset and jealous. So when he answered, "Yes, thousands," I was relieved. Very relieved. But I still felt guilty.

115

"How about you?" Stefan smiled. "Any other girls?" He laughed. "Come on, I'll never tell. You can trust me."

I don't know why — maybe because of Lisa, maybe because I'd never had any encouragement from Janicke — but I didn't tell Stefan about Janicke.

He shook his head. "Jesper, Jesper, this war had better end soon if you're determined to wait for my little sister."

"What about you?" I teased back. "Any conquests?"

He winked. "Wouldn't you just love to know!"

And that pretty much closed the subject.

Finally, we both got a few hours' sleep and then Jens called, and I set up the meeting for two p.m. at the apartment. It would be much easier for one person to get there than for all of us to get out. And it would be safer to do it before curfew.

Jens arrived in a milk van, dressed as a milkman. He had lots of white coats with him which he threw at Stefan and me.

"Thought you might want these," he suggested. "Do a little reconnaissance at the hospital."

"Right," Stefan said. "In fact, I suggest we go now and then come back here to set up our plan. Sven, you're the oldest, how about posing as a doctor? Kris and I will be with you as students."

Sven readily agreed. I could tell that he saw this as one more news story — and a really good story, at that. Janicke and Jens said they'd come along as backup, just to hang around outside the hospital, wander through the streets, and check out the German forces there.

We took Jens' van.

We all had our guns tucked into our pants, covered by our white coats or, in Janicke's and Jens' case, their jackets. It was a really warm day, hot actually. It was incredible being outdoors. The streets were jammed with people; everyone was going walking, visiting. It looked as though the whole city was on holiday. According to Sven, almost all the big businesses in Copenhagen had closed — their workers had simply walked out. Even the main bakeries had closed down. I guessed we'd all have to do without rye bread for a while.

Jens parked his van a block away and the three of us, after checking to make sure the coast was clear, got out and headed for the hospital. Stefan and I walked a little behind

Sven, since we were supposed to be his students.

The hospital had only one major entrance, and we had no idea whether we'd be stopped and asked for our identification papers. There was a small room just to the side of the entrance and I could see two German soldiers in there along with the regular security personnel. There was also a German guard on each side of the main door. I was way too hot; my hair was sticking to my neck and I felt my face must be red. But we walked past the guards with no problems at all. Stefan muttered directions to Sven and we followed him up to the surgical ward on the second floor, where we could meet some of Stefan's father's colleagues. These were the people who had hidden Stefan once, so he knew he could trust them.

There were Germans everywhere. The wards were full of wounded soldiers, and there were soldiers lounging in waiting rooms and hallways, there either to visit their friends or to get checked up themselves.

A door opened and Ebba Christensen, Stefan's father's nurse, almost walked right into Stefan. For a moment she was thunderstruck and didn't speak. Then she opened her mouth to say something, and imperceptibly Stefan shook his head. She looked at me and at Sven again. I could see she recognized me as well. I often used to drop by with Stefan when he visited his father at work — sometimes we came just to say hello, sometimes to wheedle a bit of money out of him.

"Doctor," she said to Sven, "please come this way. We've been waiting for you."

She led us into what used to be Stefan's father's outer office, her office really, and firmly closed the door, which had the name Dr. Brunn written on it. He wasn't in, however, and for the moment we were alone.

She looked at Stefan as if she couldn't believe her eyes. She was a small woman, with blond hair slowly turning grey, thick glasses and slightly crooked teeth. I remembered how she had kept a jar of candies on her desk and how she'd always slipped Stefan and me a couple, even when we were older. My eyes took in the room and yes, there was the jar, the same as ever, but it was empty. With no sugar to be found in the country it was impossible for the factories to make candy. I thought of my licorice drops and wished I'd brought them along.

"Well, Stefan," she exclaimed, "you could

knock me over with a feather. We all thought you'd got away to Sweden with your family."

"I did, Mrs. Christensen," he replied, "but now I'm back."

"I can see that," she declared, "but why on earth . . . ?"

"Well," Stefan said, "it's one of your patients."

"The Needle," she said, nodding her head.

"Yes," he answered, somewhat surprised.

"Oh, no need to be surprised." She smiled. "Everyone in the hospital knows who he is. He has a guard around him constantly. He needs surgery. They want to keep him alive so they can get more information out of him."

"When will he go to surgery?" Stefan asked.

"The day after tomorrow," she replied. "He had a bad gunshot wound in his arm. The bullet is out, but the arm is developing an infection and it may have to come off, we don't know."

"I'm here to get him out," Stefan said.

"I'll help you if I can, of course," she stated, not waiting for Stefan to ask. "But it won't be easy. He's always guarded, and he has a room of his own . . ."

"Can he walk?" Stefan asked.

"Well, yes, his legs are fine."

"Is he ever alone?" Stefan asked urgently. "Is there any time we can get to him?"

"Well . . ." She paused and thought hard. "Perhaps . . . when he goes to radiology. The guards will wait outside while he has the X-ray. The X-ray room connects with a reception area, but it does have its own door to the corridor as well. The guards always wait in the waiting room for him."

It was perfect.

"Can you get us a key?" I butted in.

She smiled at me. "I was wondering how long you'd be able to stay out of this, Jesper, letting Stefan do all the talking. Yes, I can get a key made for you. I'll do it tonight after my shift. But how can I get it to you?"

"A milkman will come to your house early tomorrow morning," Stefan told her. "Just give him the key. He'll knock five times — three quick, two long. All right?"

"Yes, fine."

"Do you know what time the Needle is going for his X-ray?" Stefan asked.

"Well, he has an appointment at two p.m. But what are you going to do about the X-ray technician?"

"When is the technician's lunch?" I asked.

"It's twelve to one, usually," she replied.

We all looked at each other.

"Is there any way," I asked, "that you could get the Needle to radiology at one o'clock, right after lunch?"

"Yes, I think I can arrange it without anyone being suspicious," she answered.

"And no one will have to know you switched the times?" Stefan said, worried that the Germans would suspect her.

"I have friends everywhere in the hospital," she replied. "And so does your father, Stefan. Don't worry. He'll be there at one o'clock the day after tomorrow. And no one will suspect anything."

"Thank you," said Stefan, holding out his hand to her. She shook it warmly. Then she shook hands with me, and with Sven, who hadn't said a word. He had unfortunately heard Stefan's and my real names. Oh well, it couldn't be helped.

Just before we left, Stefan reached into his jacket pocket and brought out another small paper bag. He took the glass lid off the candy jar and dropped in around thirty small licorices.

"Good luck," Ebba said with a smile as she opened the door.

We walked out of the hospital as easily as we

had walked in. Jens and Janicke were loitering on the other side of the street; they saw us, and soon we were all on our way back to the apartment, going over the plan as we drove.

12

The next day — Thursday — the Germans
extended the curfew from eight to eleven p.m.
in the hope of averting a wider strike. But it
was too late. As one, the people of Copenhagen
walked off their jobs. By Thursday night
patrol cars were being attacked by huge
crowds, and by Friday morning, the day of our
rescue action, the streetcars had stopped and
there was no public transportation in the city.
German army units were moved in from all
over Denmark, and they took over the public
utilities. They cut off the electricity, the gas
and the water. Dr. Best figured he'd bring the
city to its knees.

Some of the Panzer troops who had been
brought into the city set up barricades in the
main intersections. Jens told us he'd seen a

new game devised by the schoolchildren. They would run up to the Germans sitting in their tanks and ask them where they could buy raffle tickets to win the tank.

I laughed out loud when I heard that. It must have driven the Germans crazy.

We proceeded to the hospital through all this chaos. German troops were everywhere, and they often ran into mobs of hundreds of people who couldn't be budged. We had no trouble getting into the hospital — the place was a madhouse. It looked as if all of Copenhagen had been under fire the day before. Hallways were jammed with patients waiting for surgery, and every available doctor had been called in to help. They were taking only emergency cases. Our strange faces aroused no interest at all.

To add to the confusion, there were long lineups of mothers with small children, because the hospital was now the only place they could get milk. Sounds of crying, laughing and fighting came from the bored children.

We all had machine guns hidden under our white coats, and we tried not to walk too stiffly. I slipped into the first bathroom we passed on the main floor and taped a small brown parcel to the underside of the sink, then quickly caught up to the others. The hospital was running on full power, using its own generator, so we assumed the X-ray would go ahead as scheduled.

Unfortunately the waiting room was crammed with patients, and the X-ray room we had hoped would be empty over the lunch hour, so we could wait in it and then surprise the X-ray technician, was also very busy. It didn't look as if anyone had any intention of going for lunch. How were we to manage this now?

I had an idea and we huddled together for a moment, pretending to be discussing a case. The Needle would be there in fifteen minutes. Sven, as soon as he saw the patient who had been in the X-ray room leave, stalked in there with all the authority he could muster.

He nodded curtly to the technician. "I am Dr. Olsen assigned to a special patient who is to be here shortly. These are my two students. I will supervise the X-ray since it is I who will be operating. We will wait here until the patient arrives."

Well, the technician raised his eyebrows, but Sven commanded enough authority that he didn't argue. Although he probably thought it a bit strange for a doctor to supervise the X-ray personally, he couldn't find anything logically wrong with the statement. And so we waited while the nurse brought in two more patients, and then, finally, in came the Needle in his wheelchair, leaving his German guards outside in the waiting room. After the nurse had closed the door we pulled out our guns and told her and the technician to stand together. Then we tied them up. They both protested that they would be delighted to help, but we pointed out that the Germans wouldn't bother them too much if they appeared to be innocent victims.

The Needle looked at us all carefully, then winked at me.

"We meet again," he said, his voice thin, like his face. He looked terrible — pale, sweaty, wasted away.

We had to hurry. The guards would soon be suspicious and the hospital was crawling with German soldiers. If we were discovered it would be almost impossible to escape.

Sven unlocked the door to the outer hall, and I wheeled the Needle into the corridor. We started down the hall. The Germans looked at us curiously — everyone knew our famous "patient" — but no one yet saw anything wrong. At the end of the corridor Janicke met us and, pretending to be his nurse, took over pushing the wheelchair. We went down in the elevator, then along the main floor corridor, and I wheeled him into the men's washroom. I gave him the clothes that I had hidden there a half-hour earlier.

He put on a shirt and trousers and a white doctor's coat and we were ready to leave. Janicke walked on just ahead, Stefan and I flanked the Needle, and Sven trailed behind us. We chatted and walked briskly through the front doors and past the guard room, where one of Jens' friends, disguised as a delivery boy, had the guards occupied — picking up hundreds of hypodermics which he had just dropped on the floor. Parked about half a block away was Jens' van. Jens sauntered over, got in, started it up. We reached it, got in, and drove away. So far, not even an alarm had sounded.

We drove down Blegdamsvej to Østerbrogade, where another car was waiting. Stefan, the Needle and I got out and climbed into the second car. We continued straight down Østerbrogade until it changed into Strandvejen, where a taxi was waiting. We left the car, got into the taxi. In the taxi was another bag of clothes. I gave the Needle the uniform of a customs official to change into and a hat with the insignia of a customs officer.

We drove up to the quay at the little harbour at Hellerup. The day before, with Jens' help, Stefan had arranged to borrow a boat from a fisherman who often helped the resistance by ferrying people or messages to Sweden. On the boat's deck stood two resistance fighters dressed as customs officials. The Danish customs flag flew at its helm. But the first thing we saw was two German soldiers patrolling the dock, right in front of the boat. I swore to myself and hoped the whole rescue wouldn't fall apart.

I gave the Needle a small handgun, which he tucked into his pocket.

"Good luck," I said.

"Have a good trip," Stefan grinned.

He smiled back. "Thank you. You've done a fine job."

He took a deep breath, then willed himself to get out of the car with the energy and focus of a well man. He waved to us and walked right past the German soldiers, nodding to them as he passed, saying, "Good afternoon."

They nodded in reply. He continued on to the boat where the two men saluted him and welcomed him aboard. The engine started. Slowly, under the benign gaze of the German soldiers, the boat pulled out of the harbour.

"Let's get out of here," Stefan said to our driver. The driver started the car and we moved off, still keeping an eye on the boat to be sure it really got away. It was out of the harbour by the time we left the quay, and the Gestapo men were still chatting idly, watching it go.

Stefan and I relaxed our grip on the machine guns and sank back into our seats.

"Just like clockwork," I said.

We exchanged a look. It was a look of understanding, a look that said we'd just done a really good job. And behind that look was something else. I think we'd both enjoyed ourselves. It'd been exciting. It was terrific working together again. What a team we made! Look out, Germany, Stefan and Jesper are together again!

Stefan laughed out loud and then took the words right out of my mind.

"Look out, world," he declared, "Jesper and Stefan are together again!"

13

When we got back to the apartment Hanne greeted us, her face flushed, her eyes bright with excitement. We were barely in the door, still standing in the foyer, when she burst out: "I went to get bread and milk, and I was standing in line for the bakery when a black car pulled up and a man got out. The car drove away. The man took out a gun, aimed it at us, and fired. Everyone forgot about the bread. But did anyone run? Yes! But not away! They all ran over to this man, surrounded him, wrestled his gun away, and then everyone started yelling, 'Kill him, kill him.' We searched him. He had no identification papers, but lots of food ration cards!"

We knew what that meant and probably that crowd had known, too. The Gestapo had given the man food rations as payment, a gun, ammunition, and then had simply let him loose on the street. This was a convenient way for the Gestapo to terrorize the crowds.

"Well, someone got the gun, and he tried to get it back, and there was a big fight and he was shot. Then I ran. The Germans came right after that, shooting everywhere. It was mostly women, you know," she said, shaking her head, "and I'm afraid not all of them got away fast enough. When I got home I went to phone my friend Karen to tell her everything and I found the lines were dead. The operators must have gone home, too. First the gas and water and electricity, now this. If Dr. Best thinks he can bully us into giving in, he'd better think again," she declared, finally letting us move past her into the living room. "It won't work! No, it won't. He'll have to kill us all first."

Well, we certainly had a full-fledged strike on our hands. No transportation, no phones, workers all off their jobs. Had Dr. Best really thought he could make us submit by turning off our gas and water? I had always loved Copenhagen, but now I felt as though my heart would burst, I was so proud.

Janicke and Stefan volunteered to go to the reservoir for water. They each took a large bucket and set off on foot. It was a half-hour walk to the reservoir and I must admit I was a bit envious of Stefan, having her all to himself like that for a whole hour.

"It's incredible out there," Janicke exclaimed on their return, letting her bucket down with a thud so that a little water spilled over the spotless foyer floor. "It's unbelievable. They're building a huge bonfire at the end of the road, to keep the German patrols out. Look out the windows."

We all crowded over to the window in time to see a new bonfire ignite and blaze high. About half an hour after the bonfire was lit a fire truck arrived, surrounded by German troops, and the fire was put out. No sooner did the fire truck leave than people ran over to the bonfire, threw fresh things onto it — papers, furniture, anything at all — and lit it again. Soon the German troops were back, shooting at random down the street. A young woman fell, wounded. The fire truck returned, put out the blaze, and the Germans directed their machine guns down the street again. There must have been thirty or forty people out. I saw someone else hit; it looked like an older woman. The troops left, the fire truck left, and then people threw more stuff onto the pile — and lit it again. The

133

troops came back again; the fire truck came back. By that time there must have been fifty people on the street. The troops again shot their guns into the crowd, but no one would go inside. A young boy was hit; so was an old man. People cared for the wounded and carried them through to other streets, I guess to take them to the hospital. I couldn't believe my eyes, but once the fire truck left more junk was thrown on the pile — even whole doors — and it was lit again! It was late, the sun had set, and all we could see in the dark was the eerie glow of the bonfire and people's shadows dancing in the street below.

Then I heard the sound of a plane, a German plane. It was flying low, coming in close. I couldn't see it but Stefan yelled, "Hit the floor!" I threw myself away from the window onto the floor. There was gunfire everywhere as the plane strafed the street. I heard shrieks of fear, then screams of pain.

I scrambled to my feet. "We have to help."

Stefan grabbed me and pulled me down. "We are helping. We're in the resistance, we have missions to go on. We can't do that if we're dead."

The plane headed off and soon we heard sirens. We looked out. Shadows were running everywhere; mothers were calling for their children, husbands for their wives; some people were taking down part of the barricade to let the ambulances through. But as soon as the ambulances were gone, the barricade was built up again. A few diehards remained outside, their voices carrying up to us on the night air. The bonfire remained lit. And we stayed where we were. I felt so helpless and so heartsick — especially when I heard the children cry.

Suddenly the phone rang and we all almost jumped out of our skins. Sven got to the phone without too much difficulty. The room was actually quite bright with the reflected light of the bonfire.

"Yes, hello?" Pause. "Well, well, good for you. Yes, thank you. Yes, I will. Tomorrow. Yes, thanks." He hung up.

He clapped his hands, then rubbed them together. "Kris, Janicke," he announced, "you and I are back in business."

A pulse of excitement ran through me.

"Doing what? And how did that call get through?"

"Oh," he threw off nonchalantly, "I have a contact in the phone company. Got our secret line operational. We've been called to an editorial meeting."

"But we don't have a paper," I objected, "and I'm not an editor."

"We do have a paper," he declared. "And I'm a new editor for them and you're my new assistant and news reporter and Janicke is our photographer."

When he told me which paper, I was thrilled. It was the biggest and the best underground newspaper in the country. And, I couldn't help thinking, Janicke will be there, too, working with me all the time.

"Furthermore," he added, "there will be an issue tomorrow demanding an end to the curfew and the removal of the Schalburg Corps from the city before Copenhagen will go back to work. The Freedom Council is behind the demands, apparently."

I turned to Stefan, excited, but when I saw his face in the flickering light he didn't look happy.

"What is it?" I asked.

"Nothing," he replied. "I just hoped we'd work together again . . ."

My heart sank. Of course, Stefan was counting on me to do sabotage with him . . . but what a chance, to work with the people at that paper! On the other hand, I could see that reporting the sabotage wasn't as important as doing it . . . oh, I didn't know what to think or what to do.

"Do both," Janicke piped up, as if reading my thoughts.

"What?" I asked.

"Do both," she repeated. "Work with Bjørn, then write up your actions exclusively for the paper." It was odd to hear her use Stefan's cover name — and yet, I realized, I didn't even *know* her real name.

"Is it possible?" I asked Sven.

"Anything's possible," he laughed. "We make up our own rules. But now it's late, and we have a big day tomorrow. I suggest we all go to bed."

I did, and so did Sven, but Janicke and Stefan stayed up late into the night, talking. I could hear them laughing and whispering.

At first I felt jealous but then I thought to myself, "Good, if he gets to know her maybe he'll understand why I'm so crazy about her when I tell him . . . if I tell him."

Sometimes I'm so thick I surprise even myself.

14

That first meeting we had with the people running the paper, in a safe house in the centre of Copenhagen, was very exciting. I was treated with respect way beyond what I felt I deserved, and I was there when they outlined how they would write up the story containing the Freedom Council's demands to Dr. Best. The Freedom Council had decided to speak for the people of Copenhagen, to put some of this mass hysteria into a framework that would produce results. The council hadn't started the strike — it had been completely spontaneous — but they now felt that it was time to intervene. They told Dr. Best that the strike would not end until the Schalburg Corps had been removed from the city; the state of martial law ended; the water, gas and electricity restored, as well as the supply routes into the city; and there were to be no reprisals of any kind.

The council knew that the strike had to end. The Germans were getting ready to bomb the city out of existence. Already hundreds were wounded and many dead. Those black cars, now called "death cars" by everyone, raced through the streets, shooting into crowds, into open windows, cutting down men, women and children as they stood. But the council felt this rebellion should not end without the people being able to see that it had accomplished something. That would unite them in the strength to carry on the fight in different ways.

It took a few days of sparring back and forth, but on Sunday, exactly a week after Dr. Best had announced his curfew, the Germans started the water and electricity. On Monday the streetcars were on the move. On Tuesday some people went back to work. By Wednesday the Germans had agreed to the removal of the Schalburg Corps, had ended the shooting, had promised to lift the curfew immediately, and had said there would be no reprisals. So that day everyone went back to work and the strike was over. Our stories were being smuggled out to Sweden, and for that week the whole world knew how Copenhagen was fighting back.

Stefan, Jens and I had decided that we would go back to sabotage work together, and I would then write up the stories for our paper, as Janicke had suggested. On that Saturday Sven, Janicke and I were called to an editorial meeting at Bakken. I remember what a gorgeous day it was. Perfect summer weather. The sky was clear, the sun shone; in fact, it was just the day for a trip to Bakken.

Bakken is a lot like Tivoli, but with one big difference: it's on the outskirts of Copenhagen, and the fun fair and restaurant are surrounded on all sides by stately old forest. Waiting at the entrance are lines of horses and buggies, and for a price the driver will take you through the cobblestone drives that traverse the woods or, if you prefer, just down the long boulevard to the fun fair. The drivers then line up at the entrance to the fun fair to take weary people, often parents with small children, back to the entranceway.

As we drove through the city I found myself quite looking forward to our meeting at the Bøgely restaurant. Jens was taking us in his van; this time it was done up like a diaper-service truck. Stefan had decided to come along. He hated these meetings called in crowds; he thought them too dangerous. But it was often safer to be out in the open and in a big crowd. We all had our guns, and Jens and Stefan had insisted on being lookouts.

As we drove I couldn't help but notice that Janicke and Stefan were sitting very close together on the floor of the van. They spoke quietly to each other, laughed, looked in each other's eyes. I started to think back over the last week. Yes, I had often heard them late at night, talking, laughing. It finally dawned on me that they liked each other, I mean *really* liked each other. This came as an awful shock. I suddenly felt horribly jealous of Stefan and angry at Janicke. I stared at her. She was looking particularly pretty. Her long hair was loose and she had on a blue skirt and a short-sleeved white blouse. Stefan had grown very handsome and I had to admit they looked great together. I still looked seventeen, but Stefan could easily have been mistaken for a man in his early twenties. He wasn't as tall as me, but he was very well muscled and much better proportioned. I had an urge to tell him off at the first chance I got — but I realized that was impossible. After all, he assumed I was faithful to Lisa. I'd pretty much given him that impression when we talked. And I did still love Lisa, but I loved Janicke, too. But I couldn't explain that to him — not when it was his sister who was involved.

No, I could say nothing. Janicke was looking at him in a way she'd never looked at me. Never. Well, at least Stefan had good taste. She was beautiful, funny, smart. I suppose she had some faults, but I hadn't discovered them yet.

My thoughts were interrupted by our arrival at Bakken. Janicke and Stefan decided to take the buggy ride in. Jens would wait in the car. Sven and I walked down the boulevard together. We entered the fun fair, turned right past some games, and then right again into a small street of restaurants. The Bøgely was at the end of this street, and so its terrace looked out onto the boulevard. In fact, we could have entered straight from the boulevard, but we had wanted to make sure all was clear. The restaurant was well situated: there was a good view of the woods on three sides, and you could see who was coming.

The restaurant was crowded, as you'd expect on a Sunday at lunchtime, but I quickly spotted Janicke sitting at a table on the terrace with three older men. I could see Stefan strolling slowly near the buggies, on the lookout for anything suspicious.

I slipped into an empty chair beside Janicke,

and Sven sat down beside me. I had my back to the restaurant, and I could see Stefan clearly.

A man of about fifty, code name Adam, spoke. He was a senior editor.

"We want a story summarizing the strike," he began. "It should come out on Tuesday. The Freedom Council has called for two minutes of silence Wednesday at noon, to commemorate those who died in the strike. They are hoping the entire city will come to a stop. We can announce that and couple it with a summary of the entire strike."

That sounded good to everyone. He was just turning to Janicke to discuss pictures when I noticed something very strange. Stefan had taken a seat on one of the buggies, had the reins in his hand, and was turning it around. He then smacked the horses with the whip and they began to gallop over the grass straight for our restaurant. Had he gone crazy? What . . . I turned to Janicke, thinking this was perhaps a romantic escapade to impress her, but what I saw in her eyes was not laughter but fear. I whirled around and so did she. The men across from us were already on their feet. German soldiers were pouring out of the back rooms of the restaurant and out of the indoor section across the path. And in the midst of them, machine gun in hand, was the man I thought was Frederik.

For a split second the sight of him paralyzed me. Then instinct took over. The others were too scared to run and stood frozen, hands in the air, as the Germans yelled at us not to move. I grabbed Janicke's hand and we dropped to the ground. I pulled her under the table. We scrambled past Adam's legs, under another table filled with screaming, terrified people, and onto the grass which led to the boulevard. Now I knew what Stefan was doing. Somehow something had triggered his suspicions — and of course, he'd seen the Germans before we had. Janicke and I had been together at Ryvangen. I knew she felt the same way I did. We would rather be shot escaping than captured and tortured until they were ready to murder us. So we ran. For our lives.

Bullets whistled around us as the Germans gave chase. People screamed. The horses whinnied as Stefan urged them toward us. He pulled them up short just as we reached the buggy. Janicke put her foot on the step, then vaulted into the carriage. But at that same instant she screamed. Her arms flung backward, then she crumpled forward onto the seat. I leaped in after her. Stefan whipped the horses mercilessly and we galloped wildly down the boulevard. Stefan turned onto one of the side roads that led deep into the woods. The horses charged again, terrified of the gunshots, the whip, the noise. People out for leisurely strolls scattered and screamed in fright as we raced down the path, stopping for no one. Soon the sound of the guns faded away, but we knew we hadn't long before the Germans organized cars. There would be soldiers everywhere at the spot where we had parked.

I crouched down by Janicke, trying to see how badly she was hurt. Her eyes were open. She was breathing, but her breath was ragged. A red bloodstain was seeping across her crisp white blouse.

The forest was huge and deep, and for the moment I let Stefan drive us deeper and deeper into it. I tried to think. Janicke had a bullet in her back. The first thing was to get her to a doctor. Gently I stroked her hair, held her hand, prayed to God not to let her die. Don't die, don't die, I repeated to myself over and over again as we flew through the woods. There were fewer and fewer people now and finally we came to the end of the road. Stefan slowed the horses to a walk. He didn't even know Janicke had been hurt until he turned around, a grin on his face, to tell me that for the moment we were safe. His grin faded and the colour drained from his cheeks when he saw Janicke crumpled on the seat, her blouse soaked with blood. He jumped into the carriage and crouched on the floor, looking up into her face. "Turn me over," she whispered.

We did so, as gently as possible.

"I can't feel anything," she sighed. "That's lucky, isn't it?" I held her hand, tight.

"Easy." She smiled at me. "I can feel that."

"Don't worry, Janicke," said Stefan, "we'll find a doctor. We'll get you better." He put his cheek next to hers. "Don't worry. We'll get help. You're going to be all right."

She kissed his cheek and she squeezed my hand.

"Take care of each other." She closed her eyes as if she was going to have a little rest. But then her whole body shuddered and she sighed . . .

"She's fainted," I said.

Stefan put his finger on her neck to feel for a pulse. He put his head on her chest to listen for her heart. When he raised his head his cheek was covered in her blood.

"She hasn't fainted," he said. "She's died. She's dead."

146

Then Stefan and I clung to each other and cried like two little boys.

It was hard to leave Janicke. It was so hard. I knew how Stefan must feel, so I moved away and let him be alone with her. To say goodbye.

I also knew we had to get out of there, so I called Stefan away and we left Janicke behind and we ran. Somehow, I hardly remember how, we got to the station at Taarbaek, got on a train, and took it to Gilleleje. I knew of a safe house there, one we had used a lot when we were smuggling Jewish people to Sweden. It was a summer home, secluded in half an acre of wood, and yet close to trains and the road.

I found the key hidden under the front window as always, and let us in. We collapsed onto the beds and we both fell sound asleep. When I think back to it now, it seems a strange thing to do, but I don't think my body or brain could have dealt with anything else. I only wanted to sleep. And to forget. And for a few short hours I did.

15

I woke up with a start sometime in the middle of the night, for a moment not knowing where I was or why I was there. Then it all came back to me in a flood of feeling. *Janicke was dead*. I thought about how some nights, just as I was falling asleep, I'd imagined her dead, shot. And I'd imagined how sad I'd be, and yet how free, because I'd no longer have to feel guilty about loving both her and Lisa. Or sometimes I'd imagine that something had happened to Lisa. Then Janicke would confess she'd always loved me — and the two of us would live happily ever after. But it wasn't a dream any more, it wasn't a fantasy, it was real — and I didn't feel free. I only felt guilty. A little bit of me had asked for her death, to make my own life easier. I couldn't bear it.

I sat up in bed. I could hear sounds from Stefan's room. We were alone in the house; no one else was using it for the moment. I went to his room and found him crying his heart out.

"I loved her, Jesper," he sobbed. "And she loved me. She told me."

I wanted to scream, "I loved her, too." Tears sprang to my eyes, but I tried not to cry. I wanted to help Stefan, yet I didn't know what to say. So I just stood there, awkwardly, trying not to break down.

I don't know how long I stood like that — it felt like forever — until Stefan calmed down enough to speak. Finally he said, "I never should've allowed it. I knew it was too dangerous — out in the open like that. And why didn't someone check the restaurant? Someone always scouts a meeting place to make sure it's safe. What happened? How could it go so wrong?" He thought for a moment. "There must have been an informer. And that informer must've been the person who declared the place safe."

He leaped to his feet but then didn't know where to go or what to do. He kicked the bed in anger.

"Stupid. I was so stupid."

"You couldn't have done anything," I said,

sinking onto the bed, sick with grief. "Do you really think Janicke would have stayed behind just because you didn't think it was safe?"

"I should've scouted it myself."

I asked myself why *I* hadn't had a quick look around. I guess I just assumed that all precautions had been taken. And probably everything *had* been arranged very carefully — but it's hard to protect yourself from an informer.

I looked up to see Stefan studying my face. "You really cared about her, didn't you?" he said.

I nodded, incapable of saying how much I cared.

"I didn't realize — I didn't think — I mean, I thought you and Lisa . . ."

"I'm an ass," I said. "But," I added, "I still feel the same about Lisa."

Stefan sat down beside me, putting his head in his hands.

"You're not an ass," he said. He paused. "Janicke liked you a lot."

The picture of Frederik flashed through my mind.

"You know," I said to Stefan, "when I was captured, the first officer to interrogate me reminded me a lot of Frederik Holm."

"Who's that?"

"D'you remember Rosa Holm from our class? Her older brother."

"Oh yes, Rosa, of course. Yes, I remember your mentioning him."

"Well, he went away to Germany when we were around twelve and I could have sworn it was him sitting behind that desk at Dagmarhus, in a Gestapo uniform. And then today — he was there again. I think he must be in deep cover working for the resistance."

"Maybe we could find out by asking some of our contacts," Stefan suggested.

"If he's in deep cover, they won't tell us. And if he's not in deep cover . . ."

"If he's one of them?" Stefan said grimly. "Then I want him, and every other German who was there today, and I want to kill them, one by one."

I looked at Stefan, surprised. It was so unlike him. He had always hated using his gun, and he never did unless he and his partners were directly threatened. Then I realized that I had always felt that way, too. But now all I wanted was to kill anyone who was in the smallest way responsible for Janicke's murder. I wanted them all dead. I knew it was wrong, but I didn't care any more. I just didn't care.

The next morning we called our secure line

in Amager and spoke to Hanne. Jens had called; he was fine. Sven and the other three men had all been captured. They were being held in Vestre Jail. Sven had already managed to get a message out with a jail guard who was actually a well-placed resistance fighter. Sven had ditched his gun and the Germans had no proof that either he or the others were involved in anything. He was hopeful that if he could withstand interrogation, they'd have to let him go. His papers were in order; for all they knew, he was just a respectable citizen who'd gone out for lunch at Bakken.

If he could withstand interrogation . . . I shook my head and shuddered. Poor Sven. But perhaps he'd talk his way out of there. If anyone could, it was him. And his eternal optimism had obviously not left him.

Of course we all wondered who had tipped off the Germans, but we were sure it was none of our contacts. Everything seemed safe in Amager. Still, we couldn't go back there in case Sven was tortured and talked. Hanne said she was moving in with her friend Karen, and she invited us along. Karen had never been under investigation by the Germans, so we felt her apartment was a safe place to hide. It was a small apartment — one bedroom, living room, kitchen and bathroom. Stefan and I camped out in the living room, taking turns on the sofa. Jens got in touch with us there and we in turn checked in with Stefan's resistance contact.

Stefan and I were placed with a group doing railway sabotage. The Germans were using the trains to rush troops in from Norway, through Denmark to France. In Normandy they were engaged in a fierce battle with the Allies. Our orders were to delay the German troops — a vital operation if the Allies were to succeed. Often Danish prisoners were put on the trains to discourage us from blowing them up, so we had to be very careful about which trains we attacked. We couldn't completely stop the troops, but we certainly could slow them down. And we did.

I remember those months — the end of summer, fall and winter — in a kind of blur. For the first few months Stefan took terrible risks, and I had to be constantly on the watch, protecting him, cautioning him. He would plant explosives practically under the Germans' noses, often walking down the train tracks in broad daylight, carrying a lunch box filled with dynamite. He'd wait for a moment when no one was looking, put the dynamite in between the tracks, light a short fuse, then saunter away as the train chugged into sight. I would be covering him, my heart in my throat, my knees shaking. The train would blow up and we'd slip away in the confusion. I don't think Stefan cared much if he lived or died. But I cared, and I made sure I was always there watching him.

My thoughts were less on dying than on killing. I was determined to stay alive until I could get those responsible for Janicke's death. I kept wondering if Frederik was a Nazi. If he was with us, he might tell us who had done it. And then one day, a bright, warm day in early March 1945, Frederik and I met again.

By that time Sven had been released from jail; he had gone back underground and was once again putting out his own newspaper. I was working with him and Stefan, just as Janicke had suggested: I would go out with Stefan, do the sabotage, then write it up for Sven. I thought our sabotage group was getting too big. I mean, everyone wanted in now that they felt the war was almost over.

By then the Allies were pushing the Germans back across the Rhine into Germany. And of course we had to worry about infiltrators; it was hard to know whom to trust. Large roundups of resistance fighters took place in January and February, and the Germans shot lots of them. Torture got the Gestapo names of many more, until the entire resistance was in danger. The Gestapo stored all its information about resistance groups at Shellhuset. The resistance asked London to bomb Shellhuset and destroy the files, but London didn't want to because of the prisoners kept there and because they were sure there would be Danish civilian casualties. We — the resistance, that is — felt we couldn't bomb it ourselves because the reprisals against Danes would be terrible. It had to come from London. And soon. Word was out that the Gestapo was planning a very major raid on the resistance.

Anyway, in the midst of all of this Stefan and I decided to go on assignment — just the two of us. Was it only two weeks ago? We went to the movies. It was a theatre right downtown, and therefore a risky operation, but one neither of us could resist. We were dressed nicely, as if we were out for a Saturday afternoon matinée. I wore a double-breasted jacket that came down to my knees, a white shirt, baggy pants that came in tight at the ankles, a bright yellow tie, white socks, and Oxfords with incredibly thick soles because they were made out of tires. And, of course, what I called my gangster hat.

Stefan wore a long black coat over baggy pants with suspenders. He had on a gangster hat, too. All these things had been supplied by a good Danish clothier who had recently been "persuaded" to turn his entire stock over to the resistance.

Anyway, looking very spiffy, our parabellums (the small 9-mm guns with nine bullets that we carried in this type of operation) tucked into our inside pockets, we sauntered down the street to the theatre. We arrived just as the movie was starting, bought our tickets, and walked in. Stefan went to buy candy. He loitered there for a minute, as if trying to make up his mind, while I slipped upstairs. I found the projection room with no trouble and tried the door handle. I wasn't locked — which was strange, considering that we weren't the first to stage one of these little raids. There had been others a few months back. But since it had been quiet for a while, I guess they thought we'd given up. I pulled out my gun, opened the door, stepped into the small room, and greeted the terrified projectionist. From my other coat pocket I pulled a reel of film.

"I think the audience would love to see this," I remarked.

Trembling, he took it from me and stopped the reel that was playing. I could hear groans from the audience, but they waited patiently for the film to be fixed. In a moment they found themselves watching instead a parody of Hitler. As they roared with laughter, I tipped my hat and ran out the door and down the stairs. Stefan had his gun out and was covering the movie attendants, but it really wasn't necessary. They were crowded around the entrance, laughing along with everyone else. We slipped out the door and were sauntering down the street, feeling quite pleased with ourselves, when suddenly German cars were everywhere. We and everyone else on the street were caught in a Gestapo cordon.

We decided to make a run for it. We slipped into a candy store across the street from the theatre and ran out through the back exit — right into the arms of Frederik. He had soldiers placed at all the doorways, ready to intercept people like Stefan and me who were trying to avoid going through the barricades and showing their papers.

Stefan pulled out his gun and started to shoot. I did the same. I think we managed to wound a couple of them before Stefan was shot in the arm and dropped his gun. Then Frederik screamed, "Don't shoot them. I want them alive!" I was tackled by at least three big goons and my gun was knocked out of my hand. They grabbed me and cuffed me, then did the same to Stefan. I could see that his arm was oozing blood.

"Damn," Stefan said. "*Damn!*" And I know he wasn't even feeling his wound. He was only sorry that he hadn't killed all of them.

It was just bad luck, really. It wasn't that they'd been tipped off about the movie theatre; we had simply picked the wrong time to be on the wrong street.

They brought both Stefan and me here to Shellhuset. Stefan is three cells away. They took the bullet out and then they tortured him by beating him on that arm. I know because he sends me messages through the other prisoners, and sometimes we meet briefly on our morning visit to the washroom.

It's strange that the Gestapo have brought us here. The others jailed at Shellhuset are all very important members of the resistance. The Germans must think they can get some information out of us — maybe to help them in the big raid they have planned.

They've tortured me and I haven't talked. I always thought I would. The pain was excruciating. But I just said, over and over, "I have nothing to say. I have nothing to say." I thought I would die, and I didn't really mind. And now Frederik says they're going to shoot me. Well, when? What are they waiting for?

They know they've lost the war. But they'll shoot us anyway. When, I wonder, when? Why don't I mind so much? I think it's what they've turned me into. For a split second, in that alley, I saw that Stefan and I had lived on nothing but hate for months. We had turned ourselves into such balls of hate that killing had become natural. I would have killed them all with my bare hands if they'd let me.

The scary thing is, I still would.

16

I just heard from Stefan. He's doing okay, he says. He's still hoping this place'll get bombed by the British. So am I. The RAF bombed Gestapo headquarters in Aarhus in October last year, completely destroying it. Maybe the resistance will talk them into doing the same here. I'd rather die that way than be shot like a dog by those Nazis.

I've seen Frederik only once since I've been here, that time two days ago. He came in at the end of the interrogation. He said, "Please cooperate. If you don't, they will shoot you." I still don't think he recognizes me. I'm sure it's him. I can't believe he's a Nazi. He must be in deep cover. Or that's what I hope, anyway.

The rumour here is that the Gestapo now have enough information stored in Shellhuset to unravel the entire resistance organization — and that they are planning major raids. Most of the prisoners here are very high up in our organization, and they've been talking. My torture has been mild in comparison. The fellow next door had a foot brace put on his heel. Attached to it was a thin wire. They put the wire around his ankle and slowly tightened it, cutting through the skin first, then the muscle, right to the bone. He's in bad shape. They used the finger-breaker on him first. He finally broke down. I would have, too.

Anyway, if this place doesn't get blown to bits the whole resistance will end up behind bars, and they'll all be shot.

I can hear boots. I feel too tired to worry or even be nervous. It must be morning, as they've already been here with what they call breakfast — lukewarm chicory water and a piece of stale bread. It took me all day yesterday and most of the night to compose that story in my head. It got me through the worst of the pain. My hands have just a general dull ache now.

The boots have stopped at my door. Oh, God, why don't they just kill me? I'll break soon, I know it. Will they crack my fingers today? That would be unbearable, they hurt so much already. The guards open the door and yell, *"Heraus! Schnell!"*

I follow them down the hall. I hope for a glimpse of Stefan, but his door is shut. I'm taken to an interrogation room on the fourth floor.

Herr Mueller, my usual interrogator, is on the third floor. He's a baby-faced man — blond, blue-eyed, immaculately dressed, manicured nails — and he loves to give pain. He gets a fantastic thrill from it.

But no, the man seated behind the desk is not Mueller. It is Frederik.

I'm shoved into a seat facing the desk. Frederik waves the guards away. They move to the back of the room, reluctant to miss any of the fun.

"No, get out, get out," he demands, irritated. "Leave me alone with him."

They do so, but I can see they aren't pleased.

This is it. The moment of truth. Will he recognize me? If not, do I tell him? Will he help me escape? Is it really my "brother" Frederik?

He looks at me intently.

"This isn't the first time we've met, is it?" he asks. He shakes his head. "I know you . . ." And he smiles. A real smile, warm and friendly just as I remember it. "I do know you, don't I?"

And now I have to choose. Oh hell, I say to myself, I'm going to die anyway. I'll tell him who I am and I'll find out.

"It's me, Frederik," I say, "Jesper."

He looks at me for a moment, and then he recognizes me and for a split second he's incredibly happy and I almost think he's going to run over and give me a big hug, but then that look is replaced by one of horror. Horror and dismay.

"Jesper," he sighs.

"That's a fantastic cover," I say. "It's good to see you. Oh, and by the way, can you use your pull to get me out of here?" My heart is thumping. How will he react? What will he say?

He rises from his chair, claps his hands behind his back, and paces for about a minute, back and forth, behind the desk. Then he seems to come to some sort of decision. He folds his arms and looks me in the eye.

"Jesper," he says, "you gave yourself away just now, and I could have used that. I could have pretended to be in the resistance and it would have been easy for me to get all the information I wanted out of you. You would have told me everything." He pauses. "But you were always like my little brother, and I won't play games with you. This isn't a game. This is serious, it's life or death." He walks around the desk, perches on it and looks at me fondly. "I'm glad you ended up here, in this office, with me. Because I'm going to help you."

I feel totally confused. I mean, there he is, the same kind older brother, smiling at me, offering his help as always, his voice friendly but firm, except there's one major difference. He's a Nazi. And he's right: I was stupid, really stupid, giving myself away like that. Yet he isn't going to take advantage of that. He's still Frederik — open, honest, fair . . . Oh, I feel like screaming in frustration. And then I think of Janicke and suddenly all I want is to kill him. Frederik shakes his head and permits himself a small rueful laugh.

"I know what you feel right now, Jesper. I know what you think of me. But believe me, I did what I thought was for the best. It was for the good of the country. It was the best thing for Denmark."

"And it didn't hurt you either, did it?" I choke out, looking at the insignia on his uniform which show his rank as *Obersturmführer*.

"No," he says slowly, "it didn't. But you see, they recognize talent and brains and they reward them. They took me in, encouraged me, taught me, and showed me qualities in myself

I didn't know I had. They could do the same for you, Jesper. And I could help."

Well, I'm not so far gone that I can't realize what he's trying to do. He's trying to turn me. And maybe he's sincere. He must have some feeling left for me, and maybe he honestly feels he can help me. I don't think it's just a Gestapo line. On the other hand, surely he knows it's all over. They've lost. Why would I turn now? Maybe he thinks that I'll turn just to save my life and that he can get lots of information out of me that way.

Frederik picks up a silver case from his desk and offers me a cigarette. I shake my head. He lights one for himself and then gets up, brings his chair around from behind the desk, and places it close to me. He sits down and leans forward, his face earnest and intent.

"Jesper . . . look, Jesper, you've got in with one group of people, but you're young . . . have you ever thought that maybe you don't know the whole story? It's so easy to believe that the Germans are devils, are bad, are evil, and that you and the men you look up to are good. But — and just try to open your mind to this possibility — what if it's the other way around?" He leans back in his chair. "Now, I know what's going on in your mind. You feel that my thinking is all wrong, cockeyed, but what if it's your thinking that's all wrong? Yes, it's true there are some ugly things going on now and some of the people involved are in it only for money or power. But there are people like that everywhere. Don't you think some of your resistance buddies love the power?" He pauses for effect, waiting for his question to sink in.

It's true, of course, I've met some who seemed to like what they were doing, liked to be in control — maybe even liked to kill. And again I wonder if Stefan and I are turning into killers, no better than the Nazis. Something must show on my face because he nods and says, "So you know I'm right. Good. And you'll understand that I'm right about the rest, too. You see, the Aryan race has a spiritual destiny to fulfill. And we Danes are part of that Aryan race. We were helping to make one place in this world where things are pure, where everything is done with the highest ideals. We were trying to make the world a better place to live. And you, Jesper — you're bright, you're brave, you could have been part of this dream. Maybe it's still not too late."

This dream! I almost scream at him, but I don't speak; the words just race through my mind: A dream to you, a nightmare to us! What about Lisa? What about Stefan? Jews aren't part of your little dream, are they? Surely he doesn't still believe this? Doesn't he know they've lost?

I have to think fast now. I know my life depends on it. I can't afford any more stupid mistakes like the one I made when I trusted him and told myself he couldn't possibly be a Nazi. It's hard, though, because there's a feeling of hatred and fury rising in me like the huge wave that washed over me on that grey day in Amager when Frederik and I first met.

I have to make some sort of response. He's looking at me, waiting. What should it be? How I honestly feel? Then I would have to kill him. But I have to say something. I'm in a lot of trouble, and one way or another maybe he's still my ticket out of here. I decide to keep him talking until I can figure out what to do. In a strange way I feel the first hope I've had since I've been here. Maybe I can get Stefan and me out.

"Look," I say, my confusion genuine, my curiosity also very real, "how did this happen? How did you get involved?"

"A woman," he answers with a wink, man to man. "A very beautiful woman, who happens to be my fiancée now. The daughter of a very prominent Nazi general. Of course, all I knew at first was that there was this gorgeous girl who seemed to like me . . . Well," he laughs, "I was too shy to ask her out on a date — she was in my literature course — so she asked me. And after a while I was going to her home for dinner, and of course her father would talk to me, and he showed me how things really were."

"Oh," I reply, my voice tight, as I try to sound neutral, "how were they?"

"Well, he simply showed me how Hitler had taken a country which was in the worst depression imaginable — a country where you needed a barrelful of banknotes just to buy a loaf of bread, where millions were unemployed — and within a few short years turned it into one of the most prosperous, well-run countries in the world. He explained how the German people had been victimized by an international conspiracy beyond our wildest dreams, and how the Jews were responsible."

"But," I sputter, "you don't really believe that, Frederik! You're too smart to believe that."

"Jesper, Jesper," he says, shaking his head, "he showed me the facts, the figures, the *truth* of it. Of course it's hard for you to believe. It was for me at first, too. I thought he was crazy, but I soon came to see that what I thought of as crazy was just the opposite. Don't you see?" he exclaims. "You're just stuck in this one way of thinking. You have to open up and be as brilliant as I know you can be!"

Suddenly I understand how people turn, and I understand what that general did to him. I see that Frederik is really an idealist like me. He's not just a monster in a Nazi uniform; he's a person — a person who deeply believes in what he's doing. How different are we really, Frederik and me? We both fight for what we believe in; we both have to kill. If it weren't for the war we would still be like brothers. For a moment the world around me shakes and reels and nothing seems solid or true any more.

As if reading my mind, Frederik says, "We aren't that different, you and I. I don't like doing the dirty work any more than you do. And if there was no resistance," he adds, "I wouldn't have to." He says that almost wistfully, with a yearning in his voice which I know is sincere. But when he talks of "dirty work" I can't help thinking of Janicke.

"You won't have to do it for long," I say, "because soon this war will be over. And you've lost." I stand up. "Don't you get it? You've lost!"

I can feel my heart racing, my face getting hot.

"All that killing, all this torture, all the children, the lives lost, it's all for nothing. For nothing!" My voice is straining; now I'm screaming at him. "We're not the same, Frederik. I don't kill for pleasure. I don't kill innocents. I don't kill people just because they are different from me. I fight men who have no business being here, men who've taken over my country." And then it all bursts out and I lunge at him and grab his throat and scream, "You killed Janicke, you bastard. I'll kill you!"

And then everything goes black.

<u>17</u>

I wake up in my cell. The guards must've hit me over the head because I have a huge lump on the back of my skull and my head is just pure screaming pain. I don't know how long I've been out, or whether it's day or night.

I drag myself over to the wall and tap out a message.

"What time?"

"Night," is the reply. "You okay?"

"Don't know," I answer. "Bad headache."

I somehow get myself back into bed. I drift in and out of consciousness. When I'm awake I try to think about Frederik, about what happened, but my head hurts too much and it's really a blessing when I'm out. The guards come with breakfast, but I can't get out of bed to get my cup. Much to my surprise, they come in with a fresh piece of bread and hot soup with a piece of real meat floating in it. I force myself to eat even though my headache makes me feel like throwing up. I feel better after I've had the soup.

Frederik who was my hero, my older brother, the one I looked up to so much — a Nazi. And why did he try to convince me like that? He isn't stupid. He must realize it's all over. Then a thought strikes me. He liked me as much as I liked him. Maybe he wants me to see him in a good light, maybe he can't stand the thought of my hating him, maybe in some strange way he wants my approval. Well, he didn't get it, did he? Although for a second there I almost sympathized with him. Again that thought appears: How different are we? But oh, I hate him. Really hate him.

I can hear the sound of boots again. My door crashes open and I'm ordered out. I try to stand but get dizzy and fall back onto my cot. The guards grab me under each arm and they sort of pull and drag me down the corridor and down the stairs, back to Frederik's office. Well, I think, better that than Herr Mueller.

Frederik sits behind his desk.

"Out," he orders the guards.

"Sir," one says as he throws me into a chair,

"it's my duty to object. You're not safe with him."

"Are you questioning my orders?" Frederik bellows. "Now get out or I'll have your stripes!"

They get out.

I slump in the chair, unable even to focus.

"It's the girl, isn't it?" he says. "The one we found in the woods. That's why you hate me so much."

"Yes," I answer, my voice weak. "I loved her. So did Stefan. But I guess that's a word you don't understand."

Frederik smiles ruefully. "I understand only too well," he sighs. "I love my fiancée very much. I love my country. Everything I've done has been because of love."

I wish I could laugh. I wish I could dismiss what he's saying. But I know he believes it to be true.

I hold up my hands to him. "Is this done out of love, too?"

He winces. "Maybe I was wrong," he says softly. "Maybe it wasn't the right way."

"Oh," I almost laugh, the derision I feel coming out in my voice, "you feel that way now because you're losing, that's all. The war's going to end and you'll be sitting where I am now. And you're scared."

He blanches as if I've hit him. Yes, I've struck a nerve. Maybe my little outburst yesterday shook some sense into him. Maybe he finally realizes it's all over.

"Look," he says, "I'll come straight to the point. Because of what you told me, I know that the man with you is Stefan and that he's a Jew." He pauses a moment, takes a breath, plunges ahead. "I'm going to help you both escape. And I'm going with you."

For a minute I'm thunderstruck. I can't respond. Finally I say, "And how do you propose to get us all out of here?"

"It won't be hard," Frederik answers. "I'll tell them I'm taking you to Vestre Jail. We'll manage to leave the guards behind somehow. Don't worry, I'll work it out."

"And then what?" I ask. "Do we all go home?"

"No," Frederik answers, "you use your contacts to get us to Sweden."

I look at him in amazement.

"It's just a plan of yours so I'll lead you to more resistance fighters. Did you really think I'd fall for that?"

"Jesper," he says, "last night I tried my best to turn your thinking around. You're tired — exhausted. It might have worked. But it didn't. At one time I believed everything I said. In

174

fact, I still believe it. But you're right — it's over. Our little talk yesterday convinced me of that more than ever. Your reaction was that of someone on the winning side. I'm not trying to trick you. I don't want your contacts. I just want out. Now. I don't want to die. If you had turned I might not have suggested this because you would have demonstrated that we still had a chance — if men like you were willing to join us. I thought about it a lot last night and I now believe that this is the best course of action."

"Why should I believe you?" I say.

"Maybe you have no choice." He smiles at me.

"And what makes you think my contacts won't kill you rather than help you get to Sweden? For that matter," I add, "what makes you think you're safe from Stefan and me? We have more reason than anyone to want you dead."

"I didn't kill that girl."

I don't reply. I can't.

"You won't kill me because I don't believe you could."

"And Stefan?"

"He won't kill me because you won't let him. At least, that's a risk I'll have to take."

"And why should either of us agree?"

"To save the other."

I stare at him.

"If you don't, they'll continue to torture Stefan. They're already planning a session for him this afternoon. I'll tell him the same thing. You must agree in order to save each other."

I have to give him credit. He's worked it all out. He knows we'd do anything for each other. And he hopes we won't kill him. But he's thinking of the old Stefan, the old Jesper. The kids he knew before he killed Janicke. Because even if he didn't actually pull the trigger, he was there and just as responsible as if he did. I think quickly. It would be a way out. It would be a chance to kill him. Yes, a chance to kill him. And it would save us more torture, even if it didn't work and we got shot trying to escape.

But could I kill him in cold blood like that? Could Stefan? Maybe it would be better to let him squirm here, afraid, until the Allies arrive and then have him tried, and disgraced, and jailed. Maybe death is too easy.

"I want to think about it," I say.

"I'm going to talk to Stefan," he replies. "Then I'll bring you both here this afternoon. Think fast."

He goes to the door and calls the guards, and I'm dragged to my cell. I can hear them going to get Stefan. I sit. And I wait. Slowly my head starts to feel clear. Now it's just the worst headache I've ever had in my life. What will Stefan say? Probably he'll spit in Frederik's face. But maybe, like me, he'll be tempted by thoughts of revenge. And maybe — as Frederik says — he won't want me to suffer any more torture.

I have to think. If Stefan and I go with Frederik, and we kill him, does that make us the same as him? How different are we? Can I kill in cold blood the way Frederik and the Nazis have all these years? But what good will it do to stay here and die just so Frederik gets captured and punished? And maybe he'll escape anyway, without us. Of course, Stefan and I could turn him over to the resistance and let them take care of him. But is that right either, letting others do the dirty work for us? My head is spinning round and round. I have questions but no answers.

The guards are back.

They open my door and push me ahead of them, back to Frederik's fourth-floor office. Stefan is sitting there. He looks awful. His face is chalky white, covered in huge bruises; his arm is swathed in a filthy bandage; he's sweating and shivering at the same time. A chair is brought forward and I'm dumped into it.

Again, Frederik orders the guards out of the room.

"We have to leave now if we are going to do it," he says. "Many of my colleagues have just left the building to go to a funeral. This would be the best time. Well?"

The silence stretches out. I don't know whether we can trust him . . . no, I don't trust him, and yet . . . what choice is there? We all stare at each other. The silence grows and grows. I can see Frederik is becoming impatient. He is just about to speak when there is a huge crash like thunder in the courtyard outside. Stefan and I look at each other. Frederik gets up and goes to the window. The door opens and one of the guards sticks his head in.

"What was that?" he asks.

Frederik turns to answer when an incredible explosion rocks the entire room. The window blows in, shards of glass fly across the room, and half the outer wall crashes down on top of Frederik. He is almost completely buried. He didn't even get a chance to cry out. I run over to him. His eyes are open, staring. His neck must be broken. He's dead.

I look at Stefan, who's pushed himself out of his chair, then at the guard. The guard is poised, gun pointed at us, ready to kill us. But another explosion rocks the building, and for a moment the guard looks around, terrified. Stefan, who's nearest to him, kicks the gun out of his hand. I charge him and punch him in the jaw as hard as I can. He falls, unconscious. We run into the hallway. Everything is a kind of dense mist made up of brick and plaster dust, and the staircase is crammed with screaming, hysterical people. Stefan and I run to the staircase. I'm in the lead. I jump on the banister and slide, bumping over people's hands as they clutch and grab the rail. Stefan follows. We travel that way until we're on the first floor. At that point the whole stairwell gives way, crushing the men and women in it. I see a huge gaping hole in the wall, and, without stopping to think, I jump. I land hard on the cement and scramble out of the way, Stefan following. We're on the street! RAF planes are roaring overhead, dropping more bombs on Shellhuset. We run down Vesterbrogade into a small chocolate shop, then stop, trying to catch our breath. A young woman stands behind the counter. She takes one look at us and asks, "What happened?"

"The English are bombing Shellhuset," I reply.

Again she looks. Will she call the Germans? Stefan and I prepare to stop her if we must.

"Look," she says, "you two had better come with me. Don't worry," she remarks as we hesitate, "I can see where you've been — and," she adds, "it's no accident that my little shop is so close to Shellhuset. One of my jobs is to watch and report what goes on there." She turns and leads us to the entrance of an apartment at the back of the shop.

I look at Stefan. "Well?" I say.

"Let's chance it," he mutters.

So we follow her through the door and upstairs to a small one-bedroom apartment which overlooks the street. She rummages in a small chest and comes out with two guns. She puts bullets in them and hands them to Stefan and me. They're British guns. She's one of us.

She smiles. "I have to go back to the shop. Keep a sharp watch. And make yourselves at home," she adds. "There're bandages in the bathroom, and antiseptic. Perhaps you'd better fix each other up." She stares at my fingers, then shakes her head in anger.

"There's not even any point any more," she snaps. "They must do it for pure pleasure!"

She hurries out and leaves Stefan and me alone. Stefan sits down gingerly on the sofa, I

180

sink into an armchair. We put the guns down on the coffee table. It has taken a moment for the reality to sink in. I look at Stefan.

"We're free," I say.

"And he's dead," Stefan replies. He bites his lip to hold back the tears brimming in his eyes.

"I couldn't have held out any longer," he says. "I'd have told them anything, done anything. I was going to say yes to Frederik."

"I was ready to believe him, too," I reply. A flood of relief pours over me. I can hear the planes flying away now. It's probably all over.

"Let me have a look at that arm," I say to Stefan.

"No," he insists, "first your hands. Then my arm."

"All right," I agree, and he sets to work on the painful task of cleaning and bandaging my fingers. Of course, when he's finished my hands are useless for anything. But just then the young woman returns.

"Let me look at your arm," she says to Stefan, and she cleans it and wraps it in a fresh bandage.

"It isn't infected," she announces. "You're lucky. You both are," she adds.

"Are we?" I say out loud.

She looks at me quizzically. How can I explain

to this stranger how I feel? Only moments ago I was faced with a terrible decision, and then suddenly everything was decided for me. I would have gone with Frederik. And yes, he was right, I probably wouldn't have let Stefan kill him. We would have handed Frederik over to the resistance, who, no doubt, would have kept him alive and used all the information he was willing to give in order to save his own skin.

I should feel happy. I should be dancing up and down. It's a perfect movie ending to the story I'd been organizing while I was in jail: a huge rescue, planes dropping bombs, the heroes escaping. And yet I feel nothing. Just tired, defeated, let down. And the worst thing is, I suddenly realize that although our rescue has saved us from what seemed like a difficult decision, it has put us in a position where we will need to make a far more difficult choice. Do we stay in Denmark and fight, or do we get out for good, escape to Sweden? Although I didn't think so at the time, Frederik was making things easy for us.

"Are we lucky?" I repeat.

"We're alive," Stefan answers.

"Then I guess we're lucky," I say. And I mean it.

18

Our new friend, Anne — she told us her real name as it's on her apartment door anyway — is very active in the resistance. She acts as a lookout from her little shop, and she's busy working for a radio operator transmitting to Sweden. German trucks with tracking equipment are often close on the heels of the transmitters and it's very important to have at least five or six lookouts each time a message is sent. She is one of the lookouts, often just moments away from being caught.

She bustles in after closing the shop, sets to work cooking, and soon sits us down to a wonderful home-cooked meal. Real meat and potatoes. "I heard what happened," she says, "from a contact who dropped in this afternoon. Want to know?"

"Yes, of course," I say.

"Well," she comments, "it's not all good news — very mixed. There were three formations of planes. For some reason the German alarm system didn't work. That's why no sirens went off. And there was no one manning the anti-aircraft guns on top of Shellhuset. So the first formation came in and dropped the bombs right on target. But then things went wrong." She looked at her food. "One of those pilots hit a pole by the railroad tracks and smashed into a garage on Frederiksberg Allé. The smoke attracted other planes in the second formation, and although it didn't look like the target, they thought it must be, so they dropped their bombs there. A school — Jeanne d'Arc — was right next door to the garage and around eighty kids have been killed, and hundreds of others injured."

Stefan and I both gasp. This is horrible. Horrible.

"Not all the bombers made the same mistake, though," she continues. "Shellhuset has been completely destroyed. Around a hundred Germans and Danish sympathizers are dead. So far, out of thirty-five or so prisoners, twenty-five are accounted for. We're hoping for more. That's about it."

"Were many RAF planes hit?" Stefan asks.

"We don't know yet exactly, but yes, quite a number — too many. The battleship *Nürnburg* shot down some, and some went down over Liseleje."

There is a silence as we all think about those poor children . . .

"What are you two going to do now?" she asks. She looks at my hands, Stefan's arm. "Look, you can stay here for a while. You have to heal up. Then maybe we can arrange to get you over to Sweden."

I have no idea what I want to do. Go to Sweden, stay and fight, lie low till it's all over — whenever that will be. I glance at Stefan. He doesn't say anything.

"Well," she says brightly, "just let me know. In the meantime make yourselves at home. I'll run you both a nice hot bath."

A hot bath is a truly wonderful thing. I have to leave my hands out and let Stefan wash me, and I feel like a stupid baby, but it's still wonderful.

"Hey," I complain, "you got soap in my eyes."

He laughs. I get out and he towels me off. Anne has given us bathrobes which are ridiculously small; they'll have to do. She's very petite, with blond hair, brown eyes — very bright, bubbly.

Stefan also bathes and then Anne redoes his dressing. She pulls two living room chairs together for Stefan and gives me the sofa, as I'm so tall. My legs still hang well over the edge.

"What are we going to do?" I ask Stefan, after she's gone to her bedroom and we're alone. The lights are out and it's warm, peaceful, safe. "What do you want to do?"

"I don't know," he replies. "I think I've had enough."

There's a silence.

"Stefan," I begin, not quite knowing how to say this, "I hated Frederik so much I could have killed him — I would have."

"Me too," Stefan replies.

"It was wrong," I say. "We had become just like them. Full of hate."

"I know," he answers quietly.

"I don't want to kill any more," I say, and to my surprise, I can hear my voice shake. "I don't want to be a murderer." I'm crying and I can't help it. I feel as if I've gone to mush inside. "I don't even know who I am any more."

"I know who you are, Jesper," Stefan says. "And you aren't like them."

Again there is a long silence.

"Somehow," I say, "I feel that going to Sweden is wrong. I don't want to fight any more, but I don't know if I could leave."

Stefan sighs. "Same here."

"So we stay?" I say.

"We stay," Stefan replies.

Finally, I close my eyes and I begin to drift off. I see an image of Lisa and me walking hand in hand toward the roller coaster in Tivoli. I hear screams and I wince, but then I remind myself what the screams of true terror sound like. Lisa trips, bumps into a big fat man who growls. She apologizes and we both run away laughing. She's very tall now. Her long red hair gleams in the sunshine; her smile is dazzling. I kiss her. Right there in Tivoli, in front of everyone. I don't care what people think and neither does she, because we're free. We're free and we can do whatever we like, think whatever we like, be whatever we like. And so we kiss again, and then we line up to get tickets for the roller coaster ride.

* * *

It's years later, but the story I organized in my head while I was in jail won't leave me. It repeats itself over and over in my mind every night as I try to fall asleep, and sometimes I even dream it. I've decided, finally, to write everything down. Perhaps then I can start to forget.

I work full-time for a newspaper, as a reporter. Lisa is just finishing medical school. We're engaged. Stefan, like his sister, is also in medical school and is also engaged. Lisa's best friend, Susanne, had returned to Copenhagen after the war, and eventually she and Stefan fell in love.

None of us talks about the war now. We would rather not think about it. But every year, on the evening of the fourth of May, Liberation Day, we, like most other Danes, put lighted candles in our windows — and we remember Janicke and Frederik, and we hope that our children never will have to face what we faced.

ABOUT THE AUTHOR

Carol Matas is one of Canada's leading writers of historical fiction. She is particularly noted for books about the Holocaust, such as *Lisa*, *Daniel's Story* (shortlisted for the Governor General's Award and winner of the Silver Birch Award), and *After the War* (Jewish Book Award). She has also written books on other historical periods, such as *Rebecca*, *The War Within*, and *Footsteps in the Snow*, a Dear Canada book.

Carol also likes to write contemporary thrillers such as *Cloning Miranda* and its sequels, *The Second Clone* and *The Dark Clone*.

She lives with her family in Winnipeg, Manitoba.